Arthur A. D. (Arthur Albert Dawson) Bayldon

**Lays and Lyrics**

Arthur A. D. (Arthur Albert Dawson) Bayldon

**Lays and Lyrics**

ISBN/EAN: 9783744779807

Printed in Europe, USA, Canada, Australia, Japan

Cover: Foto ©Andreas Hilbeck / pixelio.de

More available books at **www.hansebooks.com**

# LAYS AND LYRICS

BY

ARTHUR A. D. BAYLDON.

LONDON
GEORGE BELL AND SONS, YORK ST., COVENT GARDEN.
HULL
J. R. TUTIN, WATERWORKS STREET
1887.

# PREFACE.

---

As many of the following pieces were written at an early age, and all of them by a youth who has just attained his twenty-second birthday, many faults and blemishes will at once be discerned, but such as they are, the Author leaves them to the public, and awaits their verdict.

A. A. D. B.

Hull, May 29th, 1887.

# CONTENTS.

———

XII.                    CONTENTS.

# CONTENTS.

# ERRATA.

---

| Page 18 | *Line* 9 | for Facinates . | *read* Fascinates |
| ,, 23 | ,, 3 | ,, Or . | ,, O'er |
| ,, 24 | ,, 18, 20 | ,, E're | ,, Ere |
| ,, 24 | ,, 11 | ,, E're | ,, Ere |
| ,, 25 | ,, 11 | ,, Little | ,, Little |
| ,, 44 | ,, 4 | ,, Nourishes . | ,, Nourisheth |
| ,, 70 | ,, 21 | ,, As . . . . | ,, Has |
| ,, 73 | ,, 13 | ,, Dazzle till the tone | ,, Dazzle, till the tone |
| ,, 74 | ,, 22 | ,, A thing of dark imaginings | ,, "A thing of dark imaginings" |
| ,, 76 | ,, 3 | ,, Excite . . . | ,, Excites |
| ,, 109 | ,, 14 | ,, Long , . . . | ,, Along |
| ,, 126 | ,, 10 | ,, Wherefor . | ,, Wherefore |
| ,, 133 | ,, 13 | ,, a Comma . | ,, a Full Stop |
| ,, 144 | ,, 21 | ,, Clear . . . . | ,, Near |

# Lays and Lyrics.

## THE INVOCATION.

SPIRIT of Nature, all sustaining Power!
Oh, harken to my voice, thou who doth wander
In the still woods at midnight's awful hour,
Clad in thy flowing robes of starry darkness,
Or when the Sun uprising from the lawn
Arrays the glorious heavens with shapes and hues,
And ever shifting shadows,—sounds the woods
With strains of sweet dissolving melody.
But, oh, sweet spirit! I have found thee most
In the swift tumbling torrent, rob'd in foam,
And girdled with a stream of circling hues.
Thine echoes have resounded thro' the dale
In the dark winter nights—mournfully sweet;
And I have listen'd till the very sound
Hath lull'd me into slumber; I have watch'd
The shapes and shadows of the deep blue sky,
The braided rainbow and the shifting clouds,

**B**

The radiant glory of the sinking sun,
The noiseless twilight with her host of stars,
And the faint peeping of the rising moon
In breathless silence, and have, musing, watch'd
And listen'd for the rustlings of thy form.
At twilight's dewy time, in the deep woods,
In search of thee my footsteps have I sped,
And I have follow'd eagerly thy steps,
Hoping to meet with thee ; but all in vain.
What mortal eyes have view'd thee as thou art ?
What mortal mind can image thee in words
As fleeting as the sun illumin'd dew ?
The painter's easel and the poet's art
Alike are frail, but oh ! if there be words —
Words which have sense and thoughts which have a being —
A being more divine, embodied with
A passionate love of all things beautiful,
What changing hues should shoot thro' thy soft cheeks ?
All lovely tints—the beauty of the sky.
The torrent's foam and ocean's majesty,
Should figure forth an image like to thee.
Then, oh, sweet spirit ! if my thrilling soul
Hath caught a harmony which is but thine,
Dissolv'd in feeble accents,—I will sing,
Entreating thee to aid me in my task,
And fill my soul with inspiration due.

# *SONNETS.*

---

## *I.*

## THE TWO WORLDS.

Sprung as from mist two rolling worlds I view'd :
  One was all beauty, delug'd in pure light,
  Peopled by shapes and visions of delight ;
The other swung a shapeless solitude,
Haunted by things which evermore must brood
  In the dim wastes of melancholy Night.
  A shadowy horror hung about the height
Of desolate steeps where footsteps ne'er intrude.

And as I gaz'd with wonder, lo ! there came
  A whisper from my spirit's inmost lair :
"Yon glorious world is thine own dream of Fame,
  Which thine Imagination paints so fair ;
And that dense orb, where mighty shadows move,
Reflects the dream Reality may prove."

## *II.*

## THE SPHINX.

ALONE upon the desert wild and bare,
　　Still gazing with thy melancholy eyes,
　　While ages sweep and empires sink and rise,
Thy mighty Image stands, whose features wear
The same fix'd look thy sculptor carvéd there.
　　No shadow falls but what thy form supplies—
　　Unchangeable as thy familiar skies
And thine eternal kingdom of despair.

Like shadows by thine Image, come and go
　　A host of curious pilgrims from all lands,
And disappear as ages swiftly flow ;
　　And then the broad and ever-burning sands
With solitude and thy still steadfast face
Break on our dreams of some forgotten race.

## III.

## THE RAINBOW.

Mysterious arch! that flingst thy flaming hues
   Athwart the barriers of the firmament
   When the fierce fury of the storm is spent !
Ethereal bow! when the wild Indian views
Thy form of light, and music caught from dews
   Of twinkling rain, and fervent sunbeams blent,
   He summons all the warriors from his tent
To worship thee with shouts and wild halloos.

For us thou art an emblem of God's love
   And mercy to the habitants of earth ;
   And the bright story of thy wondrous birth
Runs thro' our minds, when, motionless above,
   We view thy flashing hues as fresh and fair
   As when the new world's fathers saw them there.

## *IV.*

## CHATTERTON.

I STAND within a garret, almost bare,
　　But for some books, (which once did homage claim
　　From one whose soul was shrivell'd by the flame
Of Genius), a table and one chair,
And that small bed.　But, lo ! a form lies there—
　　'Tis Chatterton ! who died to win a name,
　　Whose daring soul has lit the torch of Fame
Fed by the rays of his own wild despair.

Ah me ! that form whereon the moonrays beam
　　With mellow glance that touch so lightly there
A smile, that settles like a heavenly dream,
　　And softens all the madness of despair.
Ill-fated youth, who lit thy funeral pyre
And sprang amid the flames to win thy soul's desire.

## V.

## BYRON.

BYRON ! thy soul by fits was wild and sad,
  "The Mount of Song" thou didst disdain to climb,
  Like other men, but soar'd aloft sublime,
Then sunk abash'd, as if thy spirit had
A fiend that mock'd thee in wild terror clad ;
  Like that curst Jew who liveth for all time,
  A sleepless thought, as of some secret crime,
Tormented thee till many deem'd thee mad.

  Swift as the light thy spirit caught the fire
Of ancient days, ere Greece gave birth to slaves.
  Wild were the notes that quiver'd from thy lyre,
And Athens saw thee weep o'er heroes' graves.
  For Freedom's cause thou battled and defied,
  And Greece lost an Achilles when thou died.

## VI.

## JAMES THOMSON,

AUTHOR OF "THE CITY OF DREADFUL NIGHT."

DEEP in that realm, where all things move aghast,
   I met the Bard, whose spirit did repair
   Unto that Dreadful City of Despair;
Amid a train of phantoms he came last.
I scrutiniz'd him keenly as he past:
   His face was dark with anguish, plough'd by care
   And solitary brooding.   None mov'd there
Within whose brows such hopelessness was glass'd,
   When suddenly a phantom stood by me,
   And star'd with stern, yet melancholy, eyes,
Till my limbs smote with an exceeding fear.
   I heard an awful whisper: "I am he
   Who guards the portal of this realm of sighs;
Back to thy earth, why lingerest thou here?"

## VII.

## WORDSWORTH.

A SHRINE was wrought whereever thou didst stray :
    By the blue lake, or swift brook's dancing flow,
    Or that lone tarn whose waters seem to grow
Familiar with the welkin they survey ;
Or that bold rock where hung the primrose gay,
    Or the bright hues of cloud-land's fairy bow,
    Or the wild flowers that on the laneside blow—
All found a life and language in thy lay.

Perpetual streams of thought flow'd from thy mind,
    Till Nature thought the music was her own.
Pure as the light and mighty as the wind,
    Thy stately voice roll'd with an organ tone.
Thou hast bequeath'd a diadem sublime
That all will wear who love thee for all time.

## VIII.

## THE PAINTING OF NANA.

SILENCE! for love of Heaven! I would gaze,
   With dreamy eyes, till my rapt soul has wrought
   An apparition out of its own thought—
A lovely dream to haunt me for all days.
The glamour of her beauty over-weighs
   The blissful luxury my senses sought.
   A lightning gleam of Heaven I have caught,
And sink o'erwhelm'd before its dazzling rays.

I look again, and lo! it is no dream,
   For there she lies before my raptur'd sight,
Reclining still in a descending stream
   Of fadeless glory, and of sunless light;
And my heart leaps with inborn ecstasies,
Touch'd by the beams of those immortal eyes.

## IX.

## TO A GRASSHOPPER.

Thou singest of green hills with merry tune,
  Thy voice is never silent, save in sleep ;
  Thou little mimicker, who loves to leap,
And meet the falling sunbeams of hot noon,
Till winter sinks thee in a drowsy swoon,
  Absorb'd in a soft slumber, calm and deep,
  Which ne'er is broken till the sun doth peep ;
When, suddenly, thou wakest, lo ! 'tis June !

There is a lurking sorrow in all joy,
  And thou, my little piper, art not free.
How soon may beak of cruel bird destroy
  The merry impulse of thy brimming glee.
Then trill thy voice in melodies divine,
And feast thy fill while yet the sun is thine.

## X.

## A WINTER MOONLIGHT SCENE.

As lovely as the landscape of a dream :
   This spectacle, in wild fantastic show,
   Sleeps on the eye embosom'd in pure snow.
The murmurs have departed from yon stream,
Caught by the soul of Silence, and t'would seem
   As if the very hills themselves do grow
   Into the slumber of the vale below,
That bashful lies between their forms supreme.

With saint-like grace and light of music born,
   The moon hangs dreaming from her gliding car,
And sheds a tranquil lustre o'er the scene :
More genial than the blushes of the morn,
   Or noontide heat, or evening's mellow star,
For her sweet glance beams Hope and Faith serene.

## XI.

## THE PIOUS MAN.

On noble deeds his thoughtful mind is bent,
   Living the same thro' changes, joy and pain ;
   Grateful for all the blessings that remain,
And looking on all sorrows as if sent
To tender him a gentle 'monishment
   For some neglected duty—Life is plain :
   No mysteries perplex his steadfast brain,
He trusts in God and ever is content.

And at the last his spirit spreads its wings,
   (Like some worn eagle freed from its dark cage
That swiftly from our observation springs,
   Or weary wight on a long pilgrimage
Unto his destination drawing nigh)
And finds a mansion in the realm on high.

## *XII.*

## SHELLS AND FLOWERS.

I FOUND a group of shells left by the main,
   All slumbering on the broad and sunlit shore.
   With pleasing thought I gather'd them, and bore
The treasure homewards, gloating o'er my gain.
But when I heard the lonely things complain
   My soul was fill'd with yearning to restore
   The nurslings home. I journey'd out once more
Unto the deep and flung them back again.

Another time I brought some flowers home
   And set them in some vases to admire;
But ah ! they languish'd for their soft blue dome,
   Like those lone shells that murmur'd for their sire.
Slowly they droop'd, and lost all outward pride,
I could not give them freedom, so, they died.

## TO SLEEP.

HAVE I then no charms for thee,
   Gentle Sleep,
That thou wilt not visit me
    And my senses steep?
Can I woo thee to my breast,
   Modest Sprite?
Wilt thou cradle me to rest
    This lone night?
Murmur softly, bird-like flow
Thy glad ditties, sweet and low.
Till my longing feelings know
    Love's delight!

## TO A SKYLARK.

Sweet bird of the heavens !
That soarest so high,
Like the songs of a poet
Which never can die.
In the waves of thy music
Methinks I can hear
The hymns of bright angels
Harmoniously clear.
Still soaring, still singing,
Like a soul in its flight
To its Heavenly mansion.
Thou dwindlest from sight
Far away in the heavens.
I cannot tell where,
Tho' the streams of thy music
Still fill the calm air.
But lo ! like a sunbeam,
Again I behold

Thee slowly descending
    Thro' curtains of gold.
Farewell to thee Warbler !
    Thy strain is now o'er,
And thy quick twinking figure
    These eyes view no more.
An impulse of pleasure,
    A wild burst of glee,
In my bosom is swelling,
    Sweet bird, 'tis from thee !

---

## TO THE SPIRIT OF BEAUTY.

I MET thee on Life's rugged way.
Thrice blessed be that happy day,
When first I felt thy presence fill
My soul with a poetic thrill
Which lures me on at thy sweet will.
I love to watch thee in thy home :
Thy form of brightness rob'd in foam,
Thy streaming fall of rainbow tresses
Which the soft south wind caresses
With a touch sweet Love represses.

c

# NANA.

## FROM A PAINTING BY SUCHAROUSKY.

How lovely! oh how gracefully she lies!
While beauty beams like music from her eyes!
Her robeless form which bashful Nature shows
Is sweetly laid in negligent repose;
Her drooping hair in many a lustrous fold
Streams swiftly forth like rivulets of gold,
A dream of love and innocence is there,
A fairy shape all beaming bright and fair.
She lives! she glows! she facinates my sight!
Lifts up my soul enamour'd with delight!
A heavenly hue, a rapture from on high
Beams from her limbs, and sparkles in her eye.
O Lovely One! why shouldst thou linger here
With earth-born dust when Heaven is thy sphere?

O Artist Rare! whose raptur'd soul has caught
A ray of light beyond all human thought!
Thy hand has shap'd for ever-lasting joy,
A form to love which Death cannot destroy!

## TO CUPID.

NAY, my little restless Sprite,
Sure thou wouldst not take thy flight !
Cease thy struggles ! lo ! my breast
Welcomes such a beauteous guest.

Art thou lonely, pouting Elf ?
Nay be silent, calm thyself !
Sure thou would'st not wish to roam
When delicious beams a home.

The bright blue of laughing skies
Is not brighter than thine eyes ;
And thy dimpled chin's recess
Is a glen of loveliness.

Timid fawn and twinkling bee
Restless never were like thee,
Come, Sweet, make thy pillow'd nest
In the yearnings of my breast.

I forgive thee, cruel One !
Tho' with flutters thou art gone ;
For my soul has caught bright things
From the music of thy wings.

## TO POESY.

W<small>ITH</small> thy spells thou hast enthrall'd me,
            Poesy !
From my sorrows thou hast call'd me ;
At thy presence thoughts expand.
Starts to life a fairy land :
Visions bright in soft disguise,
Cluster'd with sweet melodies,
Swiftly at thy bidding rise.

Thou art ever with us here
            Gentle Sprite !
Tho' our lives be dark and drear.
Floating softly thou dost linger
Touching lightly with thy finger
Little acts of love we cherish
Which shall never, never perish.

But, like seraph, thou canst soar,
            Mighty One !
And all secret worlds explore,
Catching shapes which never die

Rob'd in Immortality.
Calmly smiling, sweetly then
Visits thou the haunts of men.

Can our falt'ring tongues repeat—
                    Spirit Bright—
Symphonies so sadly sweet,
Which for ever more around us,
Like the rainbows which surround us,
Trailing beauty o'er the skies,
Born of thine immortal eyes,
Charming us with swift surprise ?

Thou canst with thy birds and bees—
                    Poesy !
Lighten the world's miseries !
Thou canst with thy lapse of streams
Make more beautiful our dreams !
Thou canst with thy flute-like voice
Make our spirits all rejoice ;
While thy beings more sublime
Live triumphant for all time.

## THE SONG OF THE WIND.

My home is on the mountains,
  My might is in the sea ;
But none below can ever know
  My being's mystery.
Away I fly o'er the deep blue sky—
  The clouds my servants are.
I whistle a song and drive them along
  Beneath the Eve's bright star.
I frolic o'er fell, o'er mountain and dell,
  Till Thunder joins in with my fun,
And then I repose on the pure mountain snows,
  And laugh o'er the wrecks I have done.
And often at night like some mischievous sprite
  I hover o'er city and town,
And grumble and groan, until I have blown
  Domes, temples, and cupolas down,
No master have I save One on high.
  My birthplace none can declare.

I live on the deep, in caverns I sleep ;
  But who can discover my lair ?
Or torrents and fountains o'er the cloud cleaving mountains
  I pass with a sweep and a whirl ;
O'er sweet smiling lands, o'er fierce burning sands,
  My tempest dark wings I unfurl.
In wrath or in peace my motions ne'er cease,
  My spirit can ne'er be supprest ;
Altho' I may sleep on the calm breaking deep
  My murmurs are heard still in rest.
When the heavens above wrought their rainbow of love,
  And mercy to creatures on earth,
I lifted my voice, and bade them rejoice,
  And welcome its beauteous birth.
I wrap the pure light of the Sun at his height,
  The cloudlets mine edicts obey,
With vapoury veil they gather and sail,
  And mantle his tremulous ray.
In the cataract's foam I have built me a home,
  Where Freedom and I live together,
And the forests and flowers adorn our sweet bowers
  When laughs the bright summer's weather.
But often I love like some wing-folded dove
  To kiss the wan cheeks of Despair,
'Till a fluttering smile doth hover awhile
  Which tells me that Hope is still there.

Both Childhood and Age on Sorrow's dark stage—
　For Happiness is but a dream—
Will always rejoice when they hear my glad voice
　Come dancing like waves on a stream.
Near the caverns and caves where slumber the waves
　Of Ocean when weary of play
I wander and roam beneath heaven's pure dome,
　And murmur a sweet roundelay.
Like the roll sublime of sweeping Time
　My breathings were heard long ago :
I slept in the shade e're man was made
　To be Monarch of all below.
I have winnow'd the wings of beauteous things ;
　And follow'd an angel's flight,
In the days of old when man could behold
　The heavenly seraphs of light.
I have seen the bright faces of giant races
　E're Ocean roll'd over the earth ;
And I have swept o'er each desolate shore
　E're insect or creature had birth.

# POESY.

A SINGING stream of syllables, the sound
And soul-like sense of Nature's forms around.
The beings born of music's murmurings,
Bright with the bloom of beauty, and with wings
Swift as the soft eyed Seraphim to soar
And search the heights of Speculation's shore.
The scatter'd spray by the keen senses caught
From voiceless waves that move o'er sands of Thought :
These are the emblems I would weave for thee—
Yet feeble all—sweet stirring Poesy.

---

# THE DAISY.

THE ltttle gem-lit daisy in yon nook
Smiles at its own reflection in the brook,
And seems half conscious in its robes array'd
'Twas for its own sweet beauty it was made :
It meekly lifts its graceful form on high
And basks beneath the sunshine of the sky ;
Touch'd by the dew and fondled by the breeze
Its every movement seems a wish to please.

## WINTER.

THE soul stirring music
   Of birds on the spray
Is sleeping in silence
   Till the touches of May.
The lakes are all frozen,
   The rivers are still,
And tangles mysterious
   Have fetter'd the rill.
The headlands and highlands
   Are loaded with snow,
The white skirted woodlands
   Hang brooding below.
All Nature seems gazing
   Intently on high,
Where some wing-folded cloudlets
   Half cover the sky.

# THE PAINTING OF NANA :

## A SONNET.

THE bloom of early beauty and the love
Of the world's young creation, not less fair
Than the first star that streakes the deep blue air
When pensive eve hangs brooding like a dove—
O'er the last flush of sunset—are all wove
And fashion'd in that nympholepsy there.
Those dazzling eyes of rapture, and that hair
Of lustrous gold ; those rose-tipp'd twins which move
The gazer's heart with passion strong, yet pure ;
And that unrivall'd figure half concealed
By clouds of gentle shadow, which scarce hide
The melting whiteness of her glowing side ;
And those sweet limbs of beauty—which endure
No longer their gause curtains—lie revealed.

# HURRAH FOR THE OCEAN.

HURRAH for the mighty, the glorious and free,
The mad tumbling waves of the fathomless sea!
You can love your fine woodlands that girdle your home,
But give me the sight of the snow-sparkling foam.
You can praise your grand landscapes as much as you
    please,
But give me the chant of the smooth curling seas.
I have felt the solemnity mountains inspire,
And have gaz'd with a pleasure which never could tire,
But never as yet howe'er grand they may be
Have they stirr'd up my soul like the fathomless sea.
I have heard that the notes of the bulbul are sweet,
In the land of the East with its sun-beams of heat,
Where the roses are nestling the soft humming bee,—
But give me the murmurs breath'd forth by the sea.
I have watch'd the rich sunset of Indian skies
When no cloud has o'er shadow'd its beautiful dyes;
But the tints of the heav'ns were ne'er welcom'd by me
Like the swift changing hues of a wild breaking sea.
I have heard the sweet blendings of Harmony's strain

When shadows of beauty stole soft o'er the brain,
Till my soul was exalted ; my heart throbb'd with glee ;
But give me the roar of the tempest-toss'd sea.
Then hurrah for the Ocean ! the Ocean for me,
Whose billows are chainless, whose currents are free !
I've liv'd on the waters, I've liv'd on the shore,
And which do I love ? why, the sea with its roar !

———

## LINES TO A YOUTHFUL FRIEND IN TROUBLE.

MAY thy dreams be as light as the slumber
    That floats o'er a summer-night sea.
May the joys of thy future out-number
    The wishes I waft unto thee.
May the hopes of thy life's early dawning
    Be garnished with blossoms as bright
As the flowers of spring's early morning
    When twinkling with globules of light.
Tho' the missiles of Woe now confound thee,
    Like clouds they shall soon disappear ;
And the visions of Love shall surround thee,
    And snatch from thine eyelids the tear.

Tho' I know that thou now art in sorrow
For affections torn rudely away,
Oh ! remember the smiles of to-morrow
Are heralded by tears of to-day.

———

# THE TWO KINGDOMS.

———

## PART I.—DELIGHT.

SLEEPING with a peaceful motion,
On a blue and sunlit ocean,
Flush'd with beauty and with light
Glows the island of delight.
Twinkling images of things
Like a bard's imaginings
Speak a language that is known
To the dreamer's soul alone.
Bowers of luxurious ease,
Nestled flow'rets born to please,
Whose bright pearly cups shine_through

Radiant mists of sleeping dew ;
Making sunbeams seem less bright
By their wavy robes of light,
Shedding odours so intense
That they pierce thro' every sense
With the music that floats round
Trembling with delicious sound
Of soft voices, oh ! so sweet,
That no mortal can repeat
Feeble echoes he has caught
From the vision of his thought.
He is blinded with excess
Of this island's loveliness ;
He is dazzled with the light
Bursting on his raptur'd sight ;
And his senses swiftly reel
From the images they feel,
Flashing fair from their own birth
More of heaven than of earth ;
Glowing, trembling in the beams
Of the spirit's intense dreams ;
Like a host of seraphs bright
Moving in an orb of light.
On this island, oh ! so fair,
Canopied with soft blue air ;
On this ever blooming isle

Basking 'neath the sun's pure smile ;
With their pinions dropt with gold,
Beings of celestrial mould :
Dazzling as a starry fall
Of swift light all musical
Wander in this Paradise
Never view'd by mortal eyes.—
Glimpses only can be caught
By imaginative Thought.
Oh ! that island bright and fair
Not a sorrow dwelleth there—
'Tis the kingdom out of sight,
The pure kingdom of delight.

———

PART II.—DESPAIR.

On a broad and lonely shore
Where frail shapes dwell evermore,
Cold and dismal, dark, and dreary,
And where phantoms move aweary,
Or in slumber darkly brood
In the haunted solitude,
Stands an Image wild and grim

Without shape, or form, or limb,
Sculptur'd out of massive stone
Visited by forms alone.
And its lidless, sad eyes, stare
Vacant as the stagnant air ;
And its visage darkly seen
Speaks of visions which have been—
Lovely as the rainbow's form,
Bright with fervour from the storm,
Visions and most sacred dreams,
- Swift and glorious as the streams
Of the flashing springs that glow
Like wild banners, when, with slow
Motion on his kindled way
Moves the sinking god of day
With his countenance of fire
Beaming with a soft desire
For the music which the waves
Breathe thro' their enchanted caves.
But those visions, where are they ?
Call the Past and bid it say !
Trooping sunbeams were less bright
Than those visions of delight ;
They are scatter'd,—none remain,—
Smitten by a shrouded pain.
Such have been, but ne'er to be,—
All is now deep misery ;

D

And that Image stands alone
Plung'd in sorrow not its own ;
And for ever, and for ever,
Like an overflowing river,
Never resting, never ending,
But for ever still descending,
Move the shadow'd spectres there
Haunted by a wild despair—
Ghastly features sad and cold
As the Image they behold ;
Hearts as bloodless, cheeks as wan,
As the thing they look upon ;
And for ever, and for ever,
Ceasing never, ceasing never,
Roll deep sullen waves around
That broad beach without a sound—
Waves that break without a foam,
Black as their o'erhanging dome,
Ebbing now with horrid will,
Now returning slow and chill
To that sad and lonely shore,
Frowning darkly as before.
Oh ! what mortal can declare
The strange things that slumber there ?
What unsightly creatures swim
In its waters cold and dim ?
Voiceless are its waves, ah ! me—

Voiceless as Eternity.
Never shriek of wild sea bird
O'er that lonely waste is heard—
It is silent as the shore
Which it welters evermore ;
Never mortal ever saw
That strange island without awe ;
Never night and never day—
All is gulph'd in deep dismay ;
Sunless, moonless, starless ever,
Without change or touch of weather ;
Heavy with a darkness deep,
Haunted with a dreamless sleep,
'Tis the region bleak and bare,—
The wild kingdom of despair.

## ODE TO POLAND.

LAND of the haughty and the brave,
Where Freedom's banner must not wave;
Where noble spirits silent bear
All woes and sorrows but despair;
Land where bright Freedom's star is set,
But where brave hearts are loyal yet.
Land where the summer sun-beams shine
On men whose spirits inly pine,
Crush'd by the weight of tyrant chains.
Tho' thou art rent, still hope remains.
Brave hearted Poles ! ye yet shall see
The time when Poland *shall* be free,
Tho' the Oppressor strikes ye low
And dares to taunt ye in your woe.
Oh God ! who reigns divine above,
Thine attributes are peace and love;
Then harken to this nation's cry—
Ten millions droop for Liberty !

Shall the cold hearted Russian Czar
(Sole arbiter of peace or war)
This despot hated e'en by those
Who kindred born are yet his foes ?
Shall he then fetter at his will
A nation who defies him still ?
A nation, ah ! tho' rent and worn,
And doubly crush'd with woe and scorn,
Shall make him feel what they have felt,
And deal the blows that he has dealt,
And wake from this cold apathy
To burst their shackles and be free.
Oh Poland ! tho' thy doom is woe,
Are there no heroes left thee now ?
Is Kosciusko's name forgot ?
Art grown familiar with thy lot ?
Is Freedom such a joyless thing ?
Hath the vile Russian clipt thy wing ?
Is there no hope for thee but chains ?
Must tyranny usurp thy plains ?
But lo ! I see thine eyes flash fire,
And all thy former fears expire ;
Once more I hear the battle cry—
"Forward ! advance ! oh, Liberty."
Hark to the deep drum's loud alarms,
Rebellion wakes " To arms ! to arms !"
The grey-haired patriot at the cry

Draws his keen sword for Liberty,
And all his youthful strength returns
And Freedom's fire within him burns.
The stripling starts, and swift as light
Leaps from its sheath the falchion bright.
Once more the flag of Freedom waves
O'er dauntless heroes—not o'er slaves :
A gallant front, stern, calm, and still,—
One heart, one soul, one hope, one will !

## THERE IS A LONELY ROCK.

THERE is a lonely rock that bares its form
Alike to rain, to sunshine, and to storm.
It stands like one with an uplifted eye
Staring intently on the quiet sky.
That rugged rock sends greetings from afar ;
The traveller beholds it like a star.
But drawing near it grows upon his eye
And gradually seems lifted to the sky.
The peasantry that live upon the skirt
Of that wild moor invariably assert,
'Tis near that rock the primroses first bring
The sunny pledge of the approaching spring.
The meek eyed daisy cheers its lonely place,
And sprouting grass waves homage at its base,
The dewy moss clings with a fearless pride
As if the bare rock's features it would hide.

:

## CHILDHOOD REMINISCENCES.

WHY rove my thoughts ? why do my feelings cling
To that sweet time when life was in its spring ?
Why does the silent tear bedim mine eye ?
Why yearns my soul for scenes long since gone by ?
It is not woe, nor yet can it be grief ;
For tears would minister a fond relief.
If these be not, oh ! wherefore am I sad,
And wherefore weep when all the world seems glad ?
Can I recall the prayers devoutly said ?
The loving kiss before I went to bed ?
Can I recall all that thou didst for me—
My mother dear, and not remember thee ?
Even in childhood's days my spirit felt
That I was not like those who round me dwelt ;
For I would weep, and know not why I wept,
And brood in secresy when others slept ;
And often times when with my friends at play
The tears would start, and why I could not say.

And I would leave my comrades and would roam
In some dark wood till evening drew me home.
And then, oh mother ! thou with anxious face
Wouldst clasp me in a parent's fond embrace,
And thou wouldst bid me softly to repeat
My simple prayer which time has made so sweet.
Such was my life until that awful day
The tidings brought that thou hadst past away.
Oh! how I wept as the last look I cast
On that dark case that held thy body fast !
Felt that on earth all joys were lost to me—
That I had lost my all when I lost thee.
But oh the tears in secret which I shed !—
The gushing prayers before I went to bed,
The agony as day by day roll'd past
Of praying that each one might be my last.
And oh the hours (when I was thought asleep)
I have beguil'd to think of thee and weep !
And wishing that my painful life was o'er
I'd weep and weep till I could weep no more.
And if it be, as many have averr'd
My prayers by thee, oh mother ! can be heard—
That thou canst hear each heart's dissolving moan,
That thou canst view me when I weep alone.
Oh blessed thoughts ! whose sacred springs have power
To comfort Sorrow in her saddest hour !

Oh Faith, thy light is sweeter brighter far
Than the calm lustre of yon Evening star !
Brighter thou beam'st when darkest is the night.
Clouds may conceal, but ne'er subdue thy light :
Thy cheerful ray shall guide my shattered bark,
Helpless and toss'd, 'mid billows wild and dark—
Shall cheer me on till Life's wild main is o'er
And I can land upon that distant shore
And meet thee, mother dear, to part no more.

## ODE TO THE OCEAN.

(Composed at Withernsea, March 10th, 1887).

O THOU tremendous one! whose billows roll
Triumphant from the Indies to the pole
Restless and swift as the immortal soul !—

Baring thy form unto the full round moon,
With kingly pomp and motion ; then, (as soon
When the wild Tempest blows his thunderous tune),

Robing thyself with grandeur ; thou dost tower
Frenzied with whirling madness to devour
The lonely cliffs that battle with thy power.

Oh curbless one ! have thy fierce waves a home,
To crouch at will as peaceful as thy foam ;
And then, like hungry lions, proudly roam

Lashing the beach and roaring for their prey,
Strewing the gale with shaggy locks of spray ?
Careering forth they spurn man's petty sway.

Oh tameless one! who imagest the hues
Of shifting lights and shadows, and renew'st
The rain-dissolvèd cloudlets with fresh dews,

And nourishes, with melting light and sound
The tinted shells which sleep thy shores around;
And findest food for things which leap and bound

Exultant as thy billows.  Nor doth turn
From kissing with thy hoary lip each fern
Anemone, that nestles in thine urn.

Eternal type of majesty and might!
Beaming with chasms of everfleeting light,
Or dark and dreadful 'neath the cope of night.

Oh glorious one! that sheet'st the sloping strand
With sleeky foam, then at thine orb's command
Thou rollest back thy billows lone and grand.

The deep blue skies fringed with their drapery white
Sleep softly on thy bosom all the night;
But bashful fly at the approach of light.

The wingèd Dawn trips lightly with his feet
O'er thy blue waves, which rising move to greet
The infant god that holds the light and heat,

And bow themselves in homage, and are kissed
By his pure beams all struggling with the mist,
Until the Sun uprising to assist

His glowing offspring with a brighter ray,
Floats with a whirl of music on his way
And fondles thy wild tresses all the day.

The Evening star unlocks his soft bright eye
And dartles rays of radiance, which lie
Quivering with love and splendour till they die

Touch'd by the glance of thine own Queen of night,
Who strokes thy billows bursting into light,
And shadowest her image to thy sight.

Oh mighty one! thy giant form has known
Each isle, each clime, each empire, an I each zone :
Thou sweepest all and yet thou art alone.

Boundless and swift ! thy billows once swept o'er
The startled land and vanquished every shore ;
And even now earth trembles at thy roar.

The darting swordfish and the spouting whale
Belong to thee, and to the freshn'ning gale
The nautilus uplifts his slender sail.

Beneath thy heaving waters who can tell
What curious shapes and images may dwell ?—
Creatures that gambol to the Triton's shell.

Mountains and valleys, and vast multitudes
Of shells and flowers, with coral groves and woods
Of azure gloom ; where Amphitrite broods,

Where tiny fish seek refuge from their foes,
Where the grim shark in sullen silence goes
Disturbing them in myriads from repose ;

And where, alas ! are scattered ghastly bones
And human skulls, and heaps of precious stones
Flashing with light and lustre no man owns.

All, all are thine, thou proud defiant one !
Thou rollest on, thy work is never done !
No rest for thee at setting of the sun.

Tho' ages sweep, thy billows rage and toss
Their streaming crests, and feed thine emerald moss,
Whate'er betides, thy realm sustains no loss.

Thou laughst to scorn the changes of each clime ;
Tho' empires flourish and are crushed by Time
Thou art the same—majestic and sublime ;

And as I gaze, oh Ocean! on thy breast,
A rush of thoughts rise in me unsupprest
Thou wilt roll on when I am laid to rest.

And when my name's forgotten, and my race ;
When millions more have found a resting place,
Still wilt thou roll thy billows, without trace

Of age, or aught that vanquish breathing clay.
Thou wert not made to dwindle and decay,
Alone and grand thou wilt roll on for aye.

# AHASUERUS :*

## A DRAMATIC POEM.

---

SCENE, A MOUNTAINOUS DISTRICT IN AFRICA. AHASUERUS
IS DISCOVERED LYING ASLEEP NEAR A MOUNTAIN
CATARACT. TIME, SUNRISE.

*A Voice.*

BEGONE ! begone ! thou dusky pall of night,
Appear ! appear, ye trembling beams of light.

*A Spirit, singing unseen from the torrent.*

Ye streaks of light, all hail ! all hail !
　Welcome, welcome, break of day !
The planets now are growing pale
　And soon will all have sunk away.
Sisters, sisters, lift your voices,
For earth and sky and sea rejoices.

*Chorus of Spirits from the torrent.*

All hail ! all hail ! returning light,
Dismissing to his cave the night.

---

* As this piece and the one following (Jareth's Soliloquy) were written at an
early age, the author claims the indulgence of the public for them.—A. A. D. B.

We are glad to see thee glide
O'er yon mountain's hoary side.

### A Spirit.

Sisters, sisters, let us fly
Beneath the trembling beams of light !—
Away, away, unto the sky
Among the cloudlets sailing bright.

### Chorus of Spirits.

We will! we will ! the torrent's dew
Doth sparkle on our wings of blue,
Which soon shall bear us to our home.

### Spirit.

But if some mortal should behold,—

### Chorus of Spirits.

He would but think us clouds of foam.

### Spirit.

But still our forms of wavy gold
Are not like those of earthly mould.

### Chorus of Spirits.

He would but think us rays of light
Hovering o'er the mountain's height.

### Spirit.

But if our voices should be heard ?

E

## Chorus of Spirits.

He would but think it was some bird
  Singing from its native tree
  To our sister—Liberty.

*Ahasuerus*, (awaking).

I hear sweet strains,—sweet melancholy strains,—
Unlike the sounds born of an earthly type.
How soft they hover near! arising from
I know not where, and lo! I can behold
A dazzling cloud of lovely shapes ascending
From out the torrent's foam—How beautiful!
'Tis like a rainbow-column bath'd in light;
But lo! it changes, and I can perceive
Creations of another world.   How sweet
They look upon me with their deep-blue eyes!
Ah! now they hover near me.   I will speak,
And ask them whence they come.   How near they
          float!
Beautiful Beings! what-so'eer ye are—
But spirits ye must be; for I behold
The brightness and the glory of your forms.
Oh! tell me whither do ye take your flight?
Ye are so dazzling that I cannot look
Upon ye, yet I feel that ye are near.

## *Chorus of Spirits.*

We are spirits who did dwell
In a dark forbidding dell
Till a mortal set us free
By the charm of Poesy,
And he bid us fly away
(Like the mists at break of day)
To a lovely Island, where
Sorrow, Woe, and dark Despair,
Dare not enter ; but where Love,
Joy, and tender Peace do rove
O'er its rivers and its streams
Dimpled with their own bright gleams;
Or listen to the twinkling fountains
Singing to the hoary mountains,—
So sweetly that the Echoes try
To imitate their melody.
Thither fly we, mortal, now,
Where the balmy breezes blow ;
Where the tumbling torrents roar
In its forests thick and hoar;
Where the babbling brooklets tell
Of such wondrous things that dwell
Far away where they have been
Which no mortal eye hath seen.

Thither fly we—Fare thee well !

*(The Spirits vanish in the sky.)*

*Ahasuerus.*

Ah ! they have disappeared amid the clouds
Winging their glorious way ; but still I feel
The brightness of their forms upon me, still
The melody of their sweet voices fill
The secret caverns of my haunted soul.
How beautiful the light plays on the fall
Which thund'ring rolls o'er its black shatter'd rocks
In one broad column of dark heaving waves,
Stunning the soul, yet pleasing still the eye.
But lo! another change—This misty sheet
Of ever-rising spray is taking shape,
Or moulding shapes of beauty—ah ! a form,
Distinct from life, and yet so *full* of life,
Is slowly rising in the glittering spray.
It is too beautiful to look upon,
And I am dazzled.

*A Spirit appears in the midst of the falling spray.*

*Ahasuerus.*                    Still methinks I'll speak.

Bright Spirit ! with thy glowing cheeks of beauty,
Ting'd like the crimson clouds around the waning
Sun, or th' amaranth bloom of the blushing rose,
And eyes of lustrous blue, veiled with curtains

Of sleeping foam, at whose breath the flowers
Close their petals in submitting homage;
At whose voice the warbling birds are silent,
Listening to its angelic tones entranced,
And the earth trembles with suppressèd joy.
Spirit Sublime! whose spotless bosom rivals
The Alpine snows for whiteness, and shining hair
Of dazzling gold dishevell'd in profuse
Perfection, sounding like soft strains of music
At every playful gulf of gentle wind.
Sweet Spirit! deck'd with all the lovely charms
That Nature can lavish, be pleas'd to speak.

*A pause—the Spirit remains silent.*

*Ahasuerus.*

Beautiful Image
   Of azure and gold!
My soul is enraptur'd
   Thy form to behold.
Thine eyes are for brightness
   Like stars in the blue;
But thy lips in their sweetness
   As roses I view.
And the form of thy beauty
   Is shadow'd with foam;
Which hangs as a curtain

To mantle thy home.
If the form of thy beauty
So dazzling can be
How sweet must the music
Of thy voice be to me !
Then spirit of beauty, if my quest be not vain,
Oh ! speak to a mortal, whose life is his bane.

*Spirit.*
What would'st thou, child of clay?

*Ahasuerus.*                               Beautiful Shadow !
I know not how to answer thee.   The rays
Of thy transparent beauty dazzle me :
I cannot look upon thee, for my soul
Reels with excess of thy pervading brightness.
How pale become the glaring pomps of earth
When class'd with such as thee !

*Spirit.*                               Poor thing of dust !
Dost call this beautiful which is but mist
And floating foam ?—Behold !

*Ahasuerus.*                               Ah ! what is this ?
A blaze of living glory rises up
Making the very daylight dim—Music
And foam, and dazzling streams of varied light,
Illumine these dark waters till they glow
Like waves of fire.   Whilst thy bright Image grows
Expanded in the midst of its own glory

To a colossal stature.   I am faint
And giddy with the splendour of the scene.
But what is this? thou wilt not leave me thus
Thy lovely form is fading, and thy face
Reflects no more the beauty that did show
A moment back.—Oh, spirit stay! oh stay!
Thou canst not, must not, shalt not leave me thus.

*(He rushes forward as if to clasp the shadow. The spirit vanishes amid the foam, and a voice is heard singing from the torrent.)*

*Voice from the torrent.*

Like this torrent rolling ever
   Rob'd in clouds of foam—
Rolling on—a mighty river
   To its destin'd home,
Flinging rainbow shadows, when the
   Glorious sun breaks forth,
Calmly shining 'midst the frenzy
   Of the waters' wrath—
Mortals are for ever speeding
   O'er the rocks of Life;
Some are weary and are needing
   Help amid the strife;
Some are weaving rainbow shadows
   'Neath the light of Hope;

Some are fainting 'neath the sorrows
    Which they cannot cope ;
All are drifting—all are speeding—
    To the quiet tomb,
With the landmarks fast receding
    In the deep'ning gloom.

*Ahasuerus (alone.)*

Onward still ! onward, my feeble limbs I drag
Anxious and weary.   All parts of the earth
My aching eyes at intervals have seen
From India's golden sands to Russia's shore.

## JARETH'S SOLILOQUY BEFORE THE FALL OF SODOM.

FROM AN UNFINISHED DRAMA.

———

SCENE: WITHOUT THE GATES OF SODOM.
TIME: NIGHT BEFORE THE FALL.

———

*Jareth, Lot's eldest son, alone.*

AND I must stay alone here with the stars !—
If it be solitude to be with them.
They have a hidden influence which soothes
The phantasies of my o'er-heated brain—
They are so beautiful, so calm, so bright,
And yet so mournful in their loveliness.
I love to gaze upon them ; for they fill
Me with a sadness which befits me better
Than pleasures of this earth.   How deep a hush
Doth seem to hover o'er yon city now,

Sounding sad echoes in my brooding soul.
Her beauty like a blossom soon will fade
And dwindle into nothingness—ah me !
And yet there is no shadowed portent, nor
The image of an indistinct resolve,
Save the calm sweetness of a summer's night—
There's not a sound save what some night-bird makes
Or distant waterfall; the very woods
Seem hush'd beyond their wonted solitude.
Is this a sign—the calmness of despair ?
The mute harbinger of this coming doom—
The wreck and desolation of a city,
Whose reeking embers shall ascend in clouds
And hide the sun when he shall rolling, burst
From out his ocean home on that dread morn.
How little think they now, poor feeble worms,
How near, how *very* near their end is drawing.
Perchance another night, perchance not that ;
And yet they sleep upon the very brink
Of dark Eternity, knowing it not.
And if they did, what then ? t'would be in vain
To seek for Hope when Mercy's self has fled.
What could they do but rend the skies with shrieks
And prayers, and vain entreaties, till the flames
And thunderbolts cut short their useless cries ?

Then let them die in slumber, without pain,
Nor thoughts of such, dissolvèd in sweet dreams
And visions which shall never be—at least
Not here on earth.   Their doom is sealed, and naught
On earth can save them now.   Then let them sleep ;
I would not wake them if I knew this hour
Was even now the hour of their destruction.
And is it true, or is it but a dream ?
I would it were, and yet thou shin'st O moon !
In all thy wonted splendour, shedding forth
Thy beams which of themselves are beautiful.
Athwart yon stately cupolas and domes,
That soar in all their noble loveliness,
As if to greet thee as thou roll'st along.
And can the placid majesty of night
With her most starry canopy indeed
Be but the prelude of a fearful doom?
Is there no other sign,—no threat'ning star
Predicting omens dark to those who read
Their everlasting rays ? no ! they are calm—
Calm as the solitude in which they shine,
And beautiful—more beautiful in truth
If such could be.   The heavens hold no clouds
To dim the radiant brightness of their forms.
Oh ye bright constellations ! and ye orbs

That people space, illumining this earth
With your pervading beauty, and ye heavens
So boundless in your dread magnificence,
Wherein they hold their nightly watch.  Can ye
Retain your wonted loveliness unmoved
When spirits of destruction are abroad
And only wait for their appointed time
To breathe the breath of desolation there?
Alas! and can ye thus so sweetly shine
Making more beautiful the very domes
Which soon will be destroy'd? alas! can ye,—
Most wonderful of all Jehovah's works,—
Can ye adorn the city which his wrath
Shall utterly consume? alas! ye domes,
Now gleaming in the moonlight, and ye gates
Where I so oft have sat at sunset hour,
With Zazillah—how beautiful ye look.
But ah! how soon ye will be over-thrown!—
Be but a shapeless mass, a smouldering pile,
A blacken'd spot beneath the eye of heaven:
The shame of all creation whose dark doom
Shall echo thro' unnumber'd generations—
A warning and a token from the past
That God *is* God, and sin shall not prevail.
And yet it is my home, my father's home—

The home of all I love, of those sweet ties
Which shed a brightness o'er the all-else dark
And miserable world; and if it be
That I must bid farewell and swiftly turn
My back for ever on her sculptur'd domes,
'Twill be with aching feelings.   I have lov'd
The peaceful, happy days which I have spent
Within her shining walls—her collonades,
Her sweet seclusions, where bright fountains fling
Soft rainbow-shadows in the sunny noon—
Have their familiar chambers in my soul,
And mingle fragrance with the hues of love.
Yes ! I have lov'd them all ; and my last glance
Will not be one of hatred, but of woe,
Tho' man has plung'd her loveliness in gloom
And wickedness, which must be swept away.
Oh ! man, what hast thou done ? oh ! God, can I
Revile him *now*—so near—so *very* near
His awful end.   No ! I would rather pray
For his forgiveness, if 'twas not in vain.
My prayers would not be answer'd, the decree
Of the Almighty hath gone forth, and soon,
Whether I pray or not, 'twill be fulfil!'d.
There is naught left to me except to weep,
And that I cannot, if such was my wish.
Altho' my heart is breaking, still my eyes

Will ne'er express the heaviness within.
But there is one whose soul is innocent,
Who moves alone, like some bright being of
Another world—living amid the rays
Of her own beauty—she of all should live.
I cannot warn—not even speak—concerning
The edicts of Jehovah to my sire ;
For so he hath commanded me, and I
Must that command obey, until the time
Of our departure doth arrive, and then—
Alas ! what then ? Oh God ! thou wilt not let
The innocent be punish'd with the guilty ?
Wilt thou then give me power when that time—
That awful time of our departure comes
To save this lovely being from this doom—
This over whelming doom, which is denounc'd
Against this city, and all living things
That dwell within the precincts of her walls ?
Or is thy wrath—but hush ! I hear her steps—
Alas ! how can I view those earnest eyes
Whose beaming eloquence speak more than words
Uprais'd to me ?—how can I hear that voice,
So musical in its sweet utterance,
Without confessing all ? I tremble now,
And thro' my frame an icy shiver steals
Which I ne'er felt before.—But lo ! she comes.

# THE LAST SCENE.

## A DRAMATIC FRAGMENT.

[If this drama had been continued, it was the Author's intention to depict the character of Cain from the passage, " I know not : am I my brother's keeper ?" (*Gen. chapt. iv. v.* 9), which breathes more of scorn and defiance than repentance.]

---

THE TWO ALTARS OF SACRIFICE ARE DISCOVERED WITH CAIN STANDING OVER THE DEAD BODY OF ABEL.

---

*Cain.*

    Yes, he is dead ! my brother Abel's dead !

    And I am his destroyer,—be it so !

    I neither shrink nor tremble at my deed.

    No more shall he breathe forth his orisons,

    And offer his red sacrifice to Him.

    His voice was sweet, ah ! sweeter than the birds ;

    And all the earth seemed gladden'd by his form

    Which now is pale, and cold, and motionless.

    I hated him, and even hate him now,

    Though he was kind and gentle, and so fair.

I know not why I hated him : 'twas not
Because he was more beautiful than I,
Or that his voice was sweeter ; for I deem
My strength of limb and fleetness far transcend
The loveliness and symmetry of form.
How pale he looks ! his rounded cheeks have lost
Their rose-bud tinted shadows.   Why is this?—
Why should they lose their beauty and their bloom
And settle into this pale calm repose ?
This clotty stream that stiffens his bright locks
Is deeper than the animals he slew,
To curry favour with the One above
Who spurned my gentle off'ring with contempt.
But wherefore He—

*(Lucifer suddenly stands before him and Cain recoils startled.)*

*Lucifer.*
                              Thou knowest not ! but I
Can soon enlighten thee.   Of that anon.
Thy brother Abel sleepeth there.

*Cain.*
                              Spirit !
I know thee not, nor seek to know thy name ;
Thy form and aspect are not like the spirits
My father speaks about.   Begone ! and know
I seek thee not whoever thou mayst be,
Nor fear thee tho' thou com'st from  Him above.

*Lucifer (aside.)*

How fierce and haughty are these things of clay!
Cain, I am he whom thou hast never known,
But still hast served.

*Cain.*—Served, I—what dost thou mean?

*Lucifer.*

Dost thou not see thy brother lying there?

*Cain.*

Thou mockest me. Begone! I know thee not.
Say, what hast thou to do with me?—The blood
Of him who lieth there ———

*(Stops abruptly.)*

*Lucifer.*—Was shed by thee.

(I will supply thy words.)

*Cain (surprised).*—How know'st thou this?

*Lucifer.*

Now that I have excited thy surprise
I will begone, as 'tis thy wish.

*Cain.*                           Nay, hold!

I spake abruptly when I wished thee gone—
And hastily; but go if thou dost wish,
I sought thee not!

*Lucifer.*—And yet thou servest me.

F

*Cain.*

> Never, thou proud and awful-looking shape !
> Whoe'er thou art, I neither know nor fear,
> Much less do serve.

*Lucifer.*

> Where is thy mother, Eve ?—
> For she must know her youngest born is dead—
> Why comes she not ?

*Cain (greatly agitated.)*

> My mother, oh my mother !
> I little thought when I did strike the blow
> That thou would'st suffer also.

*Lucifer.* Ah ! I see
> Thou hast repented this wild deed.

*Cain.* Repented !

> Hast thou repented of aught *thou* hast done ?
> I would that I knew who thou art and wherefore
> Thou art here : for there is that about thee
> Which speaks of something higher than thou seem'st.
> Say, who art thou ?

*Lucifer.* Why seekest thou my name ?

> Methought I heard thee say, I sought thee not.

*Cain.*

> And say it still; begone !

*Lucifer.* At thy request

    I leave thee for a season.

                    *(Lucifer vanishes.)*

*Cain (alone).* He is gone!

    And I can breathe more freely, now his form

    Of deep aud lustrous darkness strokes no more

    Mine aching eyes; but oh! how beautiful!

    How glorious! and how steadfast were his looks!

    Pride and contempt were struggling on his brow

    Of stern colossal grandeur. I could feel

    His searching glance pierce thro' me thro' and thro'.

    I saw the proud defiance of his look

    Roll into furrows of a cold disdain.

    At my command begone! But lo! a form

    Of light and loveliness is drawing near:

    His glistening locks flash like a cataract

    Of intermingling shadows and sunbeams.

    His face is like the morn or sunny noon,

    Fervent with light and purity—intense

    And terrible. A soft and fleecy flame

    Plays on his radiant and ethereal form;

    And the calm motion of his kindling steps

    Breathes melody and music to mine eyes.

    He draws more near! How dazzling are his looks!

    Serenity sleeps on his gloomless brow!

What seeks he here? he is not like the form
Of that dark haughty spirit whom I spurned.
Do they then serve the mighty One above?
They are both beautiful and girt with strength;
And yet one seems no mightier than the other.
Lo! he makes for these altars.   If it be
He comes to mock me like that haughty one,
Defiance and proud searching looks shall be
My only answer.   Ah! he has approached.

(*Michael the Archangel enters.*)

## POLAND.

Oн, Poland! Poland! birthplace of the brave!
  Noble amid the fallen! canst thou see
Thy former triumphants buried in the grave
  Of dull oblivion, and to trembling be
The slave of him who is himself not free?—
  A crumbling wreck of every laurel rent,
A voiceless Image in lone majesty,
  In pity which despair his mantle lent
And made thee what thou art—a living monument.

I hear the tramp of men! I see the light—
  The dull red glare of watch-fires on the plain.
Again doth Poland figure in the fight
  Striving to burst the tyrant's feudal chain,
  And Freedom stalks indignant in the train
Of youthful patriots, whose flashing eyes
  And knitted brows proclaim that ne'er again
Shall Europe hear their vain repeated cries;
For Freedom's watch-word now re-echoes thro' the skies.

How few ! but O ! how beautifully fair
   A noble band of heroes—who, before
Yon glorious sun hath reach'd his ocean lair
   As breathing flesh, alas ! may be no more.
   For hark ! there sounds the cannon's awful roar,
And nearer floats the trumpet's piercing call ;
   The gory clouds of Battle now do low'r,
Red grow the skies above the fiery pall
Which screens from anxious view how youthful heroes fall.


And can it be that they shall fall alone
   Upon the very soil which gave them birth ?
And can it be that we shall hear the moan—
   The lamentations of each struggling serf
Who views with streaming eyes his native turf
   No longer his ? Alas ! it cannot be
That we who call ourselves the kings of earth
   Can mutely watch their efforts to be free,
   Nor stretch an aiding hand and crush stern Fate's decree.


But there is hope, although her sun seems set :
Still sparks of Freedom burn, which Time may fan,
   Tho' to the world no sign of such as yet
Foretold what is advancing in the van

Of dark Futurity; for the soul can
    Bury from day such feelings, and conceal
Its inmost thoughts from the keen eye of man,
    Till suddenly—like some deep thunder's peal—
    To life again they leap in all their might and zeal.


Yes! Freedom's tree (tho' nourish'd in the dark,
    And water'd with Affliction,) still survives;
Deep in the breast there glows a rayless spark,
    Which still will flicker till the time arrives;
    Yes! tho' the foe with scoffing jeers deprives
The very land of succour—still the light
    Of former days illumine the soul's hives
Where Freedom's thoughts are busy—aye, in spite
Of Desolation's jar—the lamp of Hope shines bright.


But thou—oh miserable despot!—thou
    Who wield'st the sceptre of a shatter'd land,
To whose dark tyranny wan nations bow;
    The time is drawing near when from thy hand
    The bauble shall be snatched by Freedom's band;
The flag's unfurl'd, the watch-fires light the sky,
    A mighty host as countless as the sand
On yonder beach—indignant, swell the cry—
The watchword of the brave—or Death or Liberty!

And England's caught the sound! I hear the hum
    Of gath'ring armies must'ring on the plain,
The neigh of steeds, the rattle of the drum,
    And the shrill notes of many a martial strain.
    How beautiful they look !—this mighty train
With banners streaming in the face of heaven,
    Doom'd to be drench'd with the deep purple rain
Of Battle's awful thunder clouds which, driven
From the hot cannon's mouth, shall soar in masses riven.


The brooding Eagles spring from their dark lair
    On startled wing to watch the coming fray.
Once more they meet—the Lion and the Bear—
    Drawn up in War's magnificent array ;
    And overhead Death hovers for his prey,
In baffled wrath the howling Jackals stand.
    Well will the fight these scavengers repay.
The Lion stands alone amid the band,
Lashing his mighty tail, and spurning fierce the sand.

## SAPPHO.

'Tis ever thus on this foreboding shore—
    The spirit droops beneath its bonds of clay
Listless and wan, but panting still would soar
    Exultant from destruction and decay.    ·
It wrestles with its lot, and doth display
    The beauties of its bright immortal part
By moulding shapes, (that cannot pass away)
    Creations fair of soul-inspiring Art,
Too glorious for this world that woos to crush the heart.


Such dreams are not of earth, but heaven, fraught
    With an unutterable love, which, thrown
Into a language which the soul has caught
    From its own beauty, dazzle till the tone
Of their own spirit's voice becomes alone
    The music of existence, and the power
Whose influence cheers the heart with grief o'er-grown,

Even as the light of some wave-beaten tower
View'd by the sailor in the storm's most evil hour.


And yet there is a time when the soul's springs
    Become inert, and not as once they were :
When from the hues of many colour'd things
    Were fashion'd images both bright and fair ;
    For now the feelings of a cold despair
    Shadow all things with darkness, till the eye
Sees dimly o'er the ruin which is there
    Of blighted hopes, and aspirations high—
A chaos of all joys—each shatter'd link and tie


Which bound the spirit's longing, and could make
    This earth more beautiful, till all hope dies
From out the breast ; for then the heart doth break,
    And like a lightning-shatter'd oak-tree lies,
    Dreary and cold, that nothing can surprise
Its dark consuming lethargy—the bloom
    Of light and beauty shed o'er earth and skies
Is gone for ever, and an awful gloom
Enwraps those lovely tints this Life did once assume.


Thus 'burning Sappho' felt when she became
    A thing of dark imaginings, o'erwrought

By Love's tempestuous frenzy, and the flame
   Of an o'er-sweeping eloquence (which naught
   But Death itself could stupify) she sought
A lifeless peace beneath the deep-blue wave.
   But by that act a living glory caught
From other worlds ; a lustrous light which gave
A halo to that rock whence she sprung to her grave.


She is at rest in slumbers calm and deep,
   And never more will Nature hear the tone
Of her sad voice.   The deep blue billows keep
   Their treasure safe, but her wild soul has grown
   A being of all beauty.   She sleeps alone,
And never more shall her transcendant lyre
   Those soul-dissolving melodies make known
Which once would leap to life at her desire—
Now breathing sounds of woe—now burning with love's fire.


But still withal—dark prophetess !—thy name
   Shall ne'er into forgetfulness descend :
Thy hopeless passion, and thy soul of flame,
   And more than all, thy melancholy end—
   These are the rays which focus-like now blend,
Making thy name immortal ; while thy lays,

Sublimely beautiful, like sunbeams lend
A beauty and a charm to all who gaze
Enamour'd on thy song which still excite our praise.

## AMBITION.

In early youth ambition is our aim :
  This idol of our nature doth imbue
Our very lives—all other things grow tame :
  We only this distemper'd dream pursue,
  Till withering Age distracts our fancy's view—
Draws from the mind its fire, the heart grows cold
  And languid in its action ;—with the dew
Of rosy hope no more are we consol'd ;
As worthless wrecks we stand beneath such ills untold.


I gaze on Rome, the mighty, and, alas !
  A universe of ruins dimly throw
Shadows of Ages crowded in one mass,—
  Fabrics of Beauty shatter'd long ago.
  Stern Time has crushed her, and her peerless brow,
Reft of its crown, sinks drooping in distress.
  Oh ! what a moral, Rome, dost thou bestow,

Of might and pomp, and this world's littleness,
Which all the books on earth could never half express.


Ages have floated in their silent sweep,
    And multiplied the ruins of her frame ;
Havoc has wrapp'd her in a mantle deep,
    And writ her epitaph in words of flame,—
    "Behold, 'tis Rome ! the city which did claim
The homage of all nations since that day
    When thousands sprang to battle in her name—
Heroes of Glory—Romans;" but the ray
Of her tremendous might is buried in decay.


Is it not better far to have a name
    Revered and honoured in Religion's cause,
With noble thoughts and actions to proclaim
    A destiny when time itself shall pause,
    Than be the minion of the world's applause,
Whose very breath is poison ?   Is it not
    More glorious, when this heavenly spark withdraws
Its essence from this body doom'd to rot,
To know that it will fly to a far brighter spot ?

## STANZAS,

SUPPOSED TO HAVE BEEN WRITTEN BY A YOUTHFUL POET

WHO DIED OF STARVATION.

THUS far I've sung, but now my Muse takes wing,
   And from my listless fingers falls the lyre.
'Tis useless then in lowly lines to sing
   Such beauties which a sceptic would admire.
My hand is growing feeble, and the fire
   Which cherish'd me is drooping wan and low ;
For I have lost the passion to aspire
   To deeds of emulation, for the flow
Of melancholy thoughts have crush'd all joys below.


And must it be I ne'er shall sing again,
   Nor ever hear one little word of praise ?
So be it then, I will not now complain,
   Nor cherish hope that there are brighter days ;

The time has gone for sympathy to raise
  My drooping soul ; for Death has drawn too near.
I only sing in silence ; and my lays
  Are but the offsprings of dark Sorrow's tear :
  Some momentary pangs which I must learn to bear.


I feel it now—my life is nearly done,
  And I shall soon be in my narrow bed.
'Tis hard to think that all the lays I've spun
  In solitude will never once be read.
Tis harder still that no one tears will shed—
  That I shall die, and be forgotten quite.
Yes ! it is hard, when every hope has fled,
  With not one friend to make my sorrows light,
  But wander on alone beneath a starless night.


I would that I could fling away for ever
  All that I feel within me, and regain
All that I've lost.  I would that I could sever
  The meshes spun by Poverty and Pain.
  But words are naught,—'tis actions which contain
The pith of what we seek—the nameless power—
  The spiritual essence—the soft rain
That nourishes the seed—uplifts the flower,
Inspiring it to brave the storms which threatning, lower.

And thus I pass my life, the helpless prey
    Of grief, brooding in darkness with the weight
Of ceaseless vigils ; driven in dismay
    To frenzy's brink ; then wand'ring in the state
Of cold despair—the tyranny of fate ;
    Seeking without the hope to ever find
The heavenly peace which holy men relate
    Is but the only bond which e'er can bind
    The tortures of the heart, the demons of the mind.


Prepare, my soul, why wilt thou linger here ?
    Thy hopes are shatter'd, and thy friends are fled ;
And those sweet joys, which once to thee were dear,
    Have vanish'd with the unreturning dead.
How many tears in secret hast thou shed ?
    How many more, alas ! are doom'd to flow !
For sorrow's weeds now flourish in the bed
    Where Hope and Love—commingling—once did grow
    Ere Death with deadly skill his cruel shafts did throw.


The sunbeams smile, but smile to me in vain.
    Where Hope is not what pleasure can there be ?
The breezes whisper their immortal strain,
    And pleasant sounds are floating from the sea :
    All Nature revels with a sense of glee—

                                    G

Fruit, birds, and flowers, are glancing every-where,
  With lulléd music breathing fitfully
Her rippling streams o'er the enamour'd air.
But these can not console the feelings of despair !

# THE WRECK OF POMPEII.

## (A SONNET.)

THE burning sun has reached his topmost height,
And sheds his spangles on the city's towers,
And shine the hues of many-color'd flowers,
While fountains fling their streaming belts of light
In foaming sheets and rainbows flash to sight,
Enshadowed in the swift-descending showers,
The city sleeps away the noontide hours,
And all is peace.   But lo ! behold yon white
Uplifted cloud that wreathes the mountain's brow—
Ah see ! it floats towards the sunlit bay !
How red the silent crater seems to glow !—
It bursts !—oh God !—AWAKE—AWAY—AWAY !
Down sweeps the lava with a maddened roar,
Wide yawns the earth, and Pompeii's no more !

# THE POOR MAN'S COMPLAINT.

## (PUBLISHED BY THE REQUEST OF A FRIEND.)

A BARN my shelter, and some straw my bed,
My drink is water, and my food is bread.
From morn to night I wander on forlorn
Cursing the day that ever I was born.
Work there is none—at least, if such there be,
By some strange chance it never falls to me.
I must not beg, however ill I feel,
I cannot starve, and yet I must not steal.
The Poor-House now I make for in despair.
Oh God, tis full! they cannot have me there.
At once I'm seized if thro' the streets I roam,
And sent to gaol because I have no home.
Forgive me—Heaven! the darksome river's wave
Shall end my sufferings and roll o'er my grave.
One mad'ning plunge!——I'm rescued, and am tried
And punish'd for attempted suicide.

Then can you wonder at the groups you meet
Of starving wretches singing in the street ?
You keep the paupers of a foreign land,
(For every town now owns its German band,
Who, neatly clad, can beg from door to door)
And treat like dust your own deserving poor.

# THE CHRISTMAS BELLS.

THE Christmas bells are pealing—
　　How merrily they sound !
Their mellow voices flinging
　　Glad greetings all around.

For me their merry chimings
　　Bring but a sense of pain,
For pensive thoughts are stealing
　　I cannot now restrain ;

For those I've lov'd so dearly,
　　Alas ! from earth are gone,
And to these merry pealings
　　I listen here alone.

And now instead of pleasure,
　　Which I was wont to feel,
These pensive shades of sadness
　　Like phantoms o'er me steal,

## THE SWISS BOY.

Hark ! the rattle of the drum !
Lo ! our hated foes now come !
Clash of arms and trumpet's blare
Mingle on the midnight air !

Up ye brave ones and away
With your dear ones while ye may !
Now the dreaded host of France
On your hamlet homes advance.

Sounds the tramp of marching feet
In the now deserted street ;
Flash the bay'nets keen and bare
In the dim and moonlit air.

Thousands marching on as one
All in stately unison—
Marching on with martial pace,
Looms each fierce and savage face.

When, all suddenly with stride
And a bearing full of pride,
Stalks a stripling, by whose dress
Is a Switzer born, I guess !

Rudely he is seized, and bands
Soon encircle tight his hands ;
While with features stern and grim
Marshal Soult scowls down on him.

" Who art thou, and wherefore here ?
(Comes the question with a sneer)
When thy countrymen have fled
With their heroes at their head ?"

Quick with passion flash the eyes
Of the youth as he replies :
" Who art thou, and wherefore here ?
I can answer sneer for sneer.

" I'm a Switzer, nobly born,
And look down on thee with scorn,
Thou who art our country's foe,
Source of all our present woe.

" Who art *thou* ?—but thy stern face
Speaks thy cursèd name and race—

Lo ! a stripling durst defy."
"Fire !" rang the cold reply.

Flash the muskets with a glare
On the stripling standing there !
Lo ! he sinks upon the street—
His brave heart has ceased to beat.

## THE FAITHFUL HOUND.

'Tis evening, and darkness sinks fast o'er the plain ;
    The bugle now sounds for our guns to cease fire ;
Detachments are ordered to bury the slain,
    Till the notes of *reveille* shall bid them retire.

And there 'mid the carnage heap'd up on the ground,
    With his charger beneath him in awful array,
Lies the form of an ensign still watch'd by his hound
    That guards his poor corse from the fierce birds of prey.

He is licking the hand which was wont to caress ;
    Tho' all have deserted, his hound is still true ;
And the moans which are utter'd reveal his distress
    As he bends o'er those features so ghastly to view.

'Tis friendship indeed which e'en death cannot sever :
    This hound has accomplish'd what none have surpassed.
A slave to his master's commands he was ever,
    And now, as a hero, mounts guard to the last.

## KASPAR STEIN.

Poor little Kaspar !   When I think of him
My bosom swells, and oft my eyes grow dim
That one so young with strategy could mar
And hold at bay the baffled hounds of war.
It was an act that many might have done—
Our Kaspar's deed—the peasant's little son.
But what of that ? true courage is the same
In secret done, or blazon'd forth by fame.
And his was of the highest, and the tale
Can yet be heard from peasants of the vale,
Who proudly rear'd a monument to show
The love for him who first descried the foe.
But to narrate his story :'Twas the time
When Bonaparte invaded Austria's clime ;
And in the village where our hero dwelt
A strange uneasiness of fear was felt,
And sentinels were watching night and day
For the first glimpse of France's proud array.

The village hung upon a mountain side,
And near it yawn'd a ravine deep and wide
Of dark descent, spann'd by a rustic bridge
Of logs rough-hewn, cut from the mountain ridge.
The nearest town was some five miles or so,
And if the French should by the main-road go,
The little hamlet would fall in their way.
No wonder, then, each peasant felt dismay.
How strange it was that little Kaspar Stein
(Who barely yet had fourteen summers seen)
Was order'd by his father to go down
And fetch provisions from the neighbouring town.
But warn'd him first (not that he felt much fear,
For none had yet reported danger near),
To hurry and not loiter on his way
But be at home by the decline of day.
It happen'd, Kaspar on his home return
Across the hill fell in with Karl Mecurn—
A handsome little chap—a shepherd's son,
And with him Kaspar went to see his gun
Which had been newly mended, and he stay'd
As boys are wont, and with his comrade play'd.
And when at length he bid his friend good-night
The moon was up above the mountain's height ;
And a deep hush reign'd over vale and hill,

Unbroken save by some low mutt'ring rill.

With hurried step our hero strode along,

Cheering his time with fragments of a song,

When, suddenly, a silence on him fell—

His spirits sank—what story should he tell?

His father's hasty temper he well knew,

For Kaspar ne'er would tell a tale untrue.

While thinking that his freak would cost him dear,

The sound of heavy tramping caught his ear.

He check'd his speed to listen, when his eye

Saw the tall forms of soldiers moving nigh,

Whose dark-blue dress and bay'nets flashing bare,

The little chap at once told who they were.

They were the French now marching o'er the hill.

A moment, and our hero's heart grew still,

And then he thought—" if but the village knew

The wooden bridge could soon be cut in two ;"

For many a time he'd heard his father say

T'was their sole chance to keep the French at bay.

One hasty glance he cast upon the foe,

And then he ran as hard as he could go.

On, on, he ran ! At length the village light

With welcome broke upon his anxious sight.

A few more steps, the wooden-bridge is past,

And now he hails his father's cot at last.

With frantic touch he opes the cottage door,
And with the cry " The French, " sinks on the floor.
His father with a bound leaps up in haste
And quickly straps his hatchet round his waist,—
Makes for the bridge, while at his eager call
The peasants quickly muster—one and all.
Shrill ring the blows, and soon one sever'd plank
With a loud crash into the ravine sank.
A few more blows, another beam falls through,
And then another, till at length but two
Thick heavy logs, hang o'er the deep ravine;
When all at once the gleam of guns is seen.
A hoarse, stern voice is answer'd by the crash
Of the descending hatchets, when a flash
Of sudden light, close followed by a roar,
A peasant sinks with bosom drench'd in gore.
An angry yell from all his comrades broke,
And fiercer still now rang the hatchet's stroke.
Loud was the crash as with one heavy blow
The shatter'd beams fall in the pit below.
The bridge is gone ! and with exultant cries
Up the steep crags each hardy peasant flies;
And when, at length, the baffled host of France
Thro' the ravine their arduous course advance,
A range of empty cottages is all

That to the foil'd and fierce invaders fall ;
And not a sign of peasants was there seen,
For they had fled—thus sav'd by Kaspar Stein.

# A CHRISTMAS SKETCH.

'Tis Christmas Morn ! and with the spangling light
   The scatter'd spray of ice-drops on the grass,
And leafless boughs, begins to shine a-bright,
   Like twinkling images of shatter'd glass ;
   The erst hoarse brook and cascade hang a mass
Of tangled ice, and flutt'ring birdlings wing
   Their way, with quick, short twitters, for, alas !
It is a bitter winter, and the spring
Is yet afar away and, 'tis too cold to sing.

But lo ! the church's many-throated bells
   With merry tongues peal forth their welcomes loud,
How on the morn the mellow greeting swells,
   As if of their own music they are proud.
   Anon, the agèd folk whom Time had bow'd
And laughing lads and lasses trooping come,
   And soon the crumbling edifice they crowd,
While the white-bearded pastor from his home
With meditative step moves t'wards the sacred dome.

And soon the hymns of triumph rise from all,
   Shaking the ancient rafters, then a calm—
A sudden hush of silence on them fall,
   As solemnly the pastor chants the Psalm—
   The eager folk all list'ning ; now with arm
In pious awe uplifted, lo ! he kneels ;
   And as the sparks of holy zeal o'er-warm
His yearning soul, he speaks the thoughts he feels,
And thro' the stately pile his prayer for all now steals.

How beautiful is Piety like this !
   Now all is still ; the organ sinks its tone
Into a brooding born of too much bliss ;
   And the calm pastor's voice is heard alone.
   On the hill's slope, seated on mossy stone,
A stranger museth with a face forlorn ;
   And who is he with eyes which tear drops own
Garb'd like a sailor, weary, droop'd and worn.
And wherefore sheds he tears on this glad Christmas
   morn ?

The sermon now is over, and out troop
   The merry lads and lasses with bright eyes.
But all the ancient folk—a pleasant group—
   Linger awhile to con with glad surprise
   The mottoes sweet their children did devise

H

With holly cluster'd and green mistletoe
  In woven shapes and curious imageries.
Donning his coat the pastor turns to go,
And with a smile to all, moves on with footsteps slow.


Now empty is the church—the folks are gone,
  All eager to enjoy their Christmas treat ;
Only an agèd woman stays alone,
  And she on bended knees doth now repeat
A prayer for one she never more may meet :
  Her son, the idol of her heart and soul,
Perchance now toss'd where scowling tempests beat
  Their rumbling wings, and angry billows roll,
Sweeping his craft along beyond man's vain control.


And as she prays with drooping form, and eyes
  Streaming with tears she cannot now resist,
The stranger enters with soft step, and spies
  Her agèd form by the bright sunbeams kiss'd ;
Whom as he views, all suddenly a mist
  Of tears arise, and gently on a seat
He sinks with half-averted head to list
  While his head throbs with feverish love to greet
That dame who fears her son she never more may meet.

But as with falt'ring touch she 'gins to rise,
   With cautious step he leaves the holy place,
Anon she totters feebly with dim eyes,
   And shade of sadness on her careworn face,
   And hies her home with slow and shuffling pace,
Her bosom fill'd with anguish.   Yet awhile,
   Poor soul ! and thou shalt feel thy son's embrace,
And on thy furrow'd cheeks shall beam a smile
Like sunbeam playing on that church's rugged pile.

Slow to her tidy cot she doth repair,
   (Which perch'd upon the ice-girt brooklet's brink)
Arriving thence she sinketh in a chair,
   And then—forsooth—her mind begins to think,
And in a wakeful slumber her thoughts sink :
Now rambling o'er her youthful years again,
   Ere eyes were dim, and wither'd face did shrink,
But lovely all belov'd by sighing swain,
Ere budding hopes were nipt by bitter frosts of pain.

Anon her thoughts have life, and fly to him—
   Her darling, who was press'd ten years ago
By cruel men, who bound him arm and limb,
   And stifled all his moanings with a blow.
   " Ah lack-a-day ! for 'twas a deed of woe !
My lov'd one shall I ever see thee more ? "

And now, poor soul! her tears begin to flow
Afresh—when timid tap comes at the door,
That scattereth the thoughts her memory did restore.

With palsied limbs she totters—not before
    All trace of tears her shaking hands destroy,
And as a sailor's form her eyes run o'er
      Her poor old heart leaps with a sudden joy,
      And like a dream her thoughts are with her boy
Far, far away into the past are flown,
    But when the stranger doth his tongue employ
A blissful thought disturbs the agéd crone,—
A moment more, and lo, she cries "My son—My own!"

And he is in his mother's fond embrace,
    Her hoary head is nestled on his breast,
She laugheth while hot tears course down her face,
    But soon her heart a wordless prayer addrest
    To One above for sending her a guest
Who never more shall pine to go away.
    Her long-cag'd bird has found its parent's nest,
And now on knees with thankful hearts they pray
    That all may happy be on this glad Christmas day.

# FRAGMENT OF A POEM.

It was a pleasant garden, where the spray
Of the world's storms had never found its way.
Full in the midst, by light of visions shown,
The palace of our slumber stood alone,
Fill'd with the breath of rapture ; and I ween
A pride of light and beauty was there seen
To dazzle and enrich.   Not far away—
But ample for its mantle to display—
A proud colossal fountain swiftly spun
A cloud of grouping shadows from the sun.
This was a welcomed favour, and oft drew
Our happy bands to watch its sparkling dew,
And listen to its legends born of Love
Brought by the lazy sunbeams from above.
And here I trow oft was a stripling seen
At sunset moving o'er the sportive green.
He was not of our circle, though we knew
He was as gentle as the morning dew ;

And we would sometimes listen to his themes
Of Love and Hope, and all such fairy dreams.
And oft his tameless visions would, like storms,
Break from their reins and take celestial forms.

## SONG TO THE RAINBOW.

Flashing form, so fair and fleeting!
  Arching hill, and vale, and sea,
To my spirit's ear repeating
  Vows of love from Him to me.

Thou art fraught with heavenly duty
  To the erring human race;
Thou art bright with more than beauty,
  Moulded from the sun's embrace.

O thou sweet one! pure and holy,
  Breathing melody above,
How I love to watch thee, lowly,
  Till my heart swims o'er with love.

While I speak thy swift hues tremble,
  Fading, fleeting fast away.
Now the flying clouds assemble,
  And thy tints, oh! where are they?

## DESPAIR:

A SONNET.

THE other night, while lying half asleep,
  A solitary phantom came and stood
  Near to my bed, and touched me with a mood
So solemn, that I felt my heart's blood creep;
And yet forsooth, I could not choose but weep,
  Altho' I felt my hopes would be renew'd
  Which blighted were, and clotted o'er with blood,
Now rotting in a phosphorescent heap.

The clock struck four—the night began to wane,
  And daylight found me in a deep distress.
And still I watched, and still the shape was there.
  I heard the mutters of the falling rain;
And as the darkness visibly grew less,
  Then knew I 'twas the phantom of Despair.

## THY MUSIC, GENTLE MAIDEN.

THY music, gentle maiden,
  Cannot dispel dull care ;
For my soul is heavy laden
  With sorrow and despair.

The music of thy ditty,
  Coined from some noble soul,
Hath moved the springs of pity
  To flow beyond control.

To night I feel a sadness
  I never felt before,
And all thy strains of gladness
  But pierce my heart the more.

'Tis true my heart is shaken
  With Disappointment keen,
And Doubts and Fears awaken
  To throng where Hopes have been.

But vain regrets are over,
  My cherish'd dream is past,
And I at length discover
  That 'twas too sweet to last.

Then pardon me, sweet maiden,
  I cannot join thy strain ;
For my soul is heavy laden,
  And my heart is fill'd with pain.

Ye lovely stars, so beautifully bright !
   Methinks ye are sweet angels, hovering
O'er this our world, to guard us till the night
   With darkness wanes ; oh that I could but spring
Unto the realm of your deep solitude !
   Not with these bonds which round my spirit cling,
But glowing with a brightness unsubdued.
   How often, stars ! when this dull world's asleep
   In silence and alone, with thoughts too deep
For utterance, your glory have I view'd,
   Till sadness would steal o'er me and I'd weep
Tears which, alas ! must often be renew'd ;
   For I would think of thee, my mother dear !
   Why thou should'st die and leave me joyless here.

ALONE I sit by thee, O friendly fire,
And musing watch thy flickering flames expire,
While from without, at intervals, I hear
The night winds chant their anthems shrilly clear.
And now and then, upon the window pane,
With patt'ring feet resounds the beating rain.
'Tis awful now in silence to unbind
The melancholy thoughts that haunt the mind :
'Tis awful now beneath the clay's dull weight
To steer the soul through the dark gate of Fate—
To turn the key and strive to pierce the gloom
That buries deep the secrets of the tomb.

# THE BROTHERS.

As this poem was composed at an early age, it would scarcely be necessary to remind the reader that the incidents and structure are not such as the author would have worked upon at any later period.

THE sun sinks down illumining with smiles
The purple hills of Greece's lovely isles:
His glorious beams their varied hues unfold
Flooding the skies with living streams of gold ;
Serenely bright the clouds his rays imbue
And woods and glens assume a deeper hue,
Till, calmly sinking from the heavenly steep,
His glowing form is greeted by the deep,
And hov'ring there—bright streams of light expand
And dye with richer tints the circling land.
Now sweetly soft like angels whispering near
The fall of sleepy waters sooth the ear,
And tenderest sounds by wandering zephyrs made
Like rolling incense steal  long the glade.

How lovely then is sunset with its flush
Of blazing light fast fading to a blush,
Like gorgeous roses bursting into bloom :
Soft glowing lights transfluent orbs of gloom !
But oh ! how beautiful with such a scene
As now I view on Greece's isle serene,
Gigantic hills, whose rugged summits soar
Above the clouds, magnificent and hoar,
Stand out in bold relief against the sky,
In the stern robes of native majesty ;
While far away just glimmering on the sight,
But faintly seen beneath the fading light,
With the calm sweep of dignity and pride,
Reluctant rolls a river's regal tide ;
Altho' it seems, so would the eye portray
To linger still, and yet it glides away,
As deep as life, and yet as noiseless too:
It flows away and yet deceives our view,
Like some sweet dream that flies at break of day
Which haunts our soul altho' it's past away.
And is it so ?  Can this bright spot endear
No other one, do I alone stand here ?
Ah no, for see ! two youthful forms recline
Near yonder stately woodlands, that entwine
The drooping limbs in many a mazy show,

That fling fantastic images below.
The Elder seems in meditation deep,
With eyes fix'd on the sun which still did peep,
As if 'twas sorrowful to sink away,
And leave the world to darkness and dismay.
Upon his pale yet handsome face appears
The stamp of sadness far beyond his years ;
For barely twenty summers had yet shed
Their smiles and tears upon his shapely head,
Thickly adorn'd with ringlets of brown hair,
That cluster o'er a forehead high and fair.
It is a face, once seen you'd ne'er forget,
'Twould fill you with a fondness and regret,
And still you feel and yet you know not why
An awe to meet the lustre of his eye ;
For there is something in its depths of blue
Unspeakable, yet beautiful to view.
Its glance is searching, yet 'tis also calm,
Excites your love, yet fills you with alarm ;
There is a wildness there, and yet more oft,
'Tis like an angel's, spiritually soft ;
And as you gaze, with eyes that scarce can brook
The scrutiny of his thought-reading look,
You feel a hidden sympathy, and yet
You wish your eyes and his had never met.

When in repose his face a sadness wears,
Not the deep signs that scathing sorrow bears
Whose furrow'd cheeks and languid eyes betray
Too much of things which Time has swept away,
'Tis more a sadness of a pensive tone
That o'er his face a calmness there hath thrown ;
A depth of thought more fittingly to scan
With penetrating eye the thoughts of man ;
A Reader of the soul more like to find
The hidden springs and motions of the mind,
Than mingle with the pompous and the proud,
The apish coxcombs of a dizzy crowd,
Or Fashion's herd to flatter as its meet,
And 'neath an air of candour hide deceit—
A living lie, a mockery and a fraud,
Envied, caressed, spurn'd, hated and abhorr'd.
His curling lips bespeak a spirit proud,
And firmer than his tender chin avow'd.
All prove a mind that could be led—not driven,—
One that might lose, and yet deserved, a heaven.
Weak and yet strong, Love, Honour, and Despair,
Scorn and Contempt, are all concentrated there ;
Who when in wrath a friend would even fear,
But when in grief a foe would feel a tear.

A mystery which Nature can but plan
Half dust, half god, and call the riddle—man.
Far different is his comrade at his side,
Tho' by the bond of brotherhood allied.
Sunburnt his face, with eyes of lightsome grey,
And mouth where sunny smiles are seen to play.
Who are they, then ? kind Reader, prythee, wait,
I cloak their names, and mission, and estate,
Enough to know from England's shore they hail ;
For thereon hangs the moral of my tale.

Now the last tints of the expiring day,
In silent streams, dissolving sink away,
And darkness reigns around, while far on high
Those mystic lights illuminate the sky,
While in the East slow rising into sight
The moon appears and sheds a mellow light.
The distant hills like giants now frown o'er
The lovely scene they beautified before.
The hours roll on, and from the heavenly height
In cloudless glory beams the Queen of Night :
Amid her starry court she calmly sails,
Flooding with glorious light the hills and dales.
Lakes, streams and brooklets own her sparkling glance,
And softly smile as her bright moonbeams dance

I

More lovely now than when the tide of day
In living wavelets slowly ebb'd away;
So tall the trees, which sentinel-like, stand
In silent groups, a dark and weird band;
So calm the plains with dusky herbage spread;
So stern the crags that darkling hang o'er head;
So bright the waves that leaping on the shore
Dance in the caves with a melodious roar:
So sweet those notes that pierce the solitude
Like some lost spirit wailing in the wood;
Now low and sad they calmly steal along
Lulling the night with their pathetic song,
Now swelling clear, but full of music still,
Each grot and cave with melody do fill,
Until it rolls in one unbroken strain,
And bursts in living music o'er the plain.
'Tis strange, but true, that even this bright spot
Is not exempt from Crime's deep-crimson blot,
For even now in yon deep vale below
Enacts a scene where Mercy dare not go,
But sighing flies and bids a long farewell
To that bright spot which man now makes a hell.
And can it be, where all is bright and fair,
That Passion lurks and finds its victims there?
On such a spot angelic forms might deign,

As in past days, to visit earth again,
So purely beautiful, so calmly bright,
A Paradise of splendour and delight.
Must such a vale of loveliness and bliss—
Ah no ! —The Fiend would love a spot like this.
It cannot be ! Vice dare not venture near,
'Tis Innocence alone who nestles here.
The Gods of Love and Beauty mingling twine
Enchantment's weo and make this spot divine ;
So would Romance with swelling raptures sing,
But stern Reality reigns o'er a string.
Sad are the notes and dreary is the strain,
Yet I must sing the Truth, tho' link'd to Pain.


Deep in that vale, amid a scene so fair,
A brigand chief hath made his secret lair,
A fierce dark crew—the terror of the land—
Outlaws from youth compose his savage band ;
Dark deeds are theirs, and many an awful tale
Each gossip-swain tells of that mountain vale,
And trembling points with many a mutter'd prayer
To some rude cross which he had planted there,
Marking the spot where he himself had seen
Dark streaks of blood upon the verdant green,

Sad witnesses—red Murder had left there,
. Speaking alike of vengeance and despair.


And those two youths—why should they linger where
Dark Horror broods and Terror find his lair?
Away! away! ye foolish ones, away!
The night draws on, 'tis danger there to stay.
They rise, they move with footsteps ling'ring yet
With pleasing awe, half mingling with regret;
The elder starts; a whistle loud and shrill
Sounds from afar and all again is still.
A moment more, and dusky forms arise,—
Spring from the grass before their startled eyes:
Tall stalwart forms with levell'd muskets stand
With scowling miens, a wild and threat'ning band.
A moment's pause, a cry of deep despair
Rings shrilly out upon the midnight air,
Then, pale and motionless upon the ground
Lie that unhappy pair—close gagg'd and bound.


Deep in a cave where never sunbeams pry,
Helpless and weary those two brothers lie,
Not knowing, but that every hour which past
So swiftly by, perchance may be their last,

That every step at intervals rings by
May be the step to take them forth to die.
Caught in the toils of a fierce brigand, they
Can only for deliverance now pray,
And wildly wish that by some strange event
A heavenly angel may at last be sent.

Bright breaks the morn, another day's began,
Another day of grief or joy for man.
It matters not, which one will be his lot—
A few short years and it will be forgot !
'Tis thus we live, thro' scenes of joy and woe,
Till we descend where all of flesh must go ;
A stone o'er-writ breathing some friend's despair,
Stands o'er the spot of all that we once were.
Not so the morn, her glorious beams are shed
O'er earth and sea—what cares she for the dead ?
She shines but for the living, therefore, man !
Partake of joys while yet thy bosom can.
Hark to the music which the skylark sings
As to the light of morn he spreads his wings ;
Gaze on yon hills that solemnly uphold
Their haughty crests from whence the darkness roll'd ;
Look at the flowers, the trees that o'er you spread
A leafy canopy to shield your head ;

Look at all these, then, tell me, canst thou say
Thy puny race deserves to live a day ?
With stormy pride thou revel'st for an hour,
And fondly deems Creation owns thy power ;
With haughty tread thou shak'st the startled earth,
And dares to snatch the secrets of her birth—
When, lo ! the soil thou fondly deem'st thy slave—
O wondrous sight !—allows thee but a grave.

'Tis noon, and still to them no news has come,
They question, but their jailers act as dumb.
Oh who can tell the agonies that they
Did undergo as slowly past the day ?
Oh who can paint ('tis far beyond my power)
The fearful torments of each cankering hour ?
'Tis passing strange— are they to live or die ?
Why speak they not ? and Echo answers, why ?
But hark ! the tramp of footsteps drawing near,
How beat their hearts with sudden hope and fear !
But lo ! it grows more distant,— dies away,
And leaves them gulph'd in silence and dismay.
'Tis night ! and all is still, save when the sound
Of the sentry's footsteps breaks the peace around ;
Save when some tuneless night-bird from the hill
A moment shrieks, and all again is still.

All are at rest save in that cavern where
Recline the forms of that unhappy pair.
Sad sight it is to gaze in and behold
Them lying there, where all is dark and cold.
The Younger is asleep, if it be sleep
To lie thus motionless, sunk in a deep
And listless stupor which speaks more of death,
Save for those heavy sighs, that deep drawn breath ;
His head is pillow'd on his brother's breast,
Who like a guardian angel soothes his rest ;
O'er his blue eye no slumber draws his veil,
Awake he lies with features calm and pale.
Where are his thoughts ? but they are far away—
A martyr's dreams are not more bright than they ;
He murmurs something softly, 'tis a prayer,
And 'tis for him—his brother sleeping there !
He prays for God to watch him, and to keep
Him from all harm, while he reclines asleep.
And now a kiss is gently printed on
Those boyish cheeks that look so pale and wan,
A ling'ring kiss, a mother's lips would give
Her dying child, which soon would cease to live.
But lo ! the sound of voices echoes near ;
Why starts he with a more than mortal fear ?
He mutters something softly, and his eye

Is lifted up as searching for the sky.
What views he there ?—'tis but the rugged rock
Which scowling down upon him seems to mock.
Away ! such thoughts ; these lifeless lumps of stone
Stem but the view of these dim eyes alone.
The spirit's glance is ever fix'd on Him
And roves uncurb'd tho' fetter'd be each limb.

The morn is up, and birds are on the wing,
Those artless bards that only live to sing.
Ah, happy ones ! they never know neglect,
Or on the rocks of hidden cares are wreck'd.
'Tis true they sometimes perish, and oft fall
A victim to the sportsman's hissing ball ;
But even when his gun he swiftly raises
His victim's heart is brimming o'er with praises;
And its last notes are but a strain of love
Which shall not fall, but rise to Him above.
Lo ! up the many windings of the glen
Arm'd to the teeth there rides a band of men,
No ransom bring they but their shining swords,
Eager for fight when heart with heart accords.
No hope of Mercy, Pity long since fled,
Now stern Revenge and Justice reign instead.
No more shall blood of helpless victims stain

Th' indignant soil of that endearing plain.
Alas! alas! why came they not before?
Too late! too late! the deed of blood is o'er.
A few hours earlier on, led out to die
A noble youth, who now a corse doth lie.

Fierce is the conflict, for each brigand knows
No quarters will be given,— these are foes
Equipped with arms which Discipline can wield,
And bearing scars from many a battle field,
Men who have stood unflinching at their post
Dauntless and cool tho' fighting 'gainst a host—
Men who have faced all dangers without fear,
And grimly smiled when even Death seem'd near,
Men who have fought when every hope seem'd fled,
And corses made the rolling stream run red,
Wounded and hopeless, yet too proud to yield,
While still their arms their sweeping swords can wield.
With back to back the savage brigands stand
Defiant still, tho' dead is half their band.
They strive to charge, to break the threat'ning foe,
And slash and thrust is answer'd blow for blow,
They waver, totter, rally and unite—
A moment more, and they are in full flight.
Exultant now and flushed with their success

Up the steep path the hardy victors press,
While some remain to search the brigand's lair
And seize whatever booty might be there.
But what is this outstretch'd upon the ground?
A human form— a stripling gagg'd and bound,
"Off with his bonds—('tis quickly done) now bear
Him gently forth into the open air.
Here on this sward recline him, softly, now
Wipe off this dew that hangs upon his brow.
But lo! he murmurs something—list ye!—hush!
Ah! he revives, his cheeks have caught a blush.
Here, give him this? 'twill rouse him— lo! a start,—
He opes his eyes." Ah, Reader, not a heart
But beats with sorrow when they heard his tale,
And not a cheek but suddenly turn'd pale
With wrath and indignation. Listen then,
The story he delivers to these men.


" This very morn my brother was shot dead,
My lot was death and yet he died instead.
I knew not this, would that I'd never known,
'Till I awoke and found myself alone.
No more I know, save what my jailer said.
Alas! that he my brother was shot dead.
Last night he heard the brigand chief had sworn

That one of us should die at break of morn.
So he went forth and gave his life, lest I
Should be the one to suffer and to die.
They led him out to die at his request.
He woke me not—oh God !—you know the rest."

A sudden hush falls on them as they hear,
And many an eye betrays a silent tear,
Some scarce believe the story they have heard,
While others ponder o'er it word by word ;
Some move away in silence, and a few
Of tender heart can scarce the tears subdue,
While there are some who out of pity press
To sooth the lad now weeping in distress.
But what is that yon group of men have found—
A human form outstretch'd upon the ground.
Why strive they thus to hide it ? 'tis in vain—
The boy looks round, and with a cry of pain
Sinks breathless down upon that bloodstain'd breast,
Gushing with tears which cannot be supprest.
'Tis he, his brother's corse whom they have found
With bosom torn with many a cruel wound.
Beautiful he lay, as if e'en Death
Had since repented his mad work ; a breath
Of fitful wind play'd with his curly hair,

And kiss'd those cheeks so delicately fair.
A gentle smile still rested on his face
As if his spirit yet retain'd its place,
So calm and still that you might almost deem
Him buried in the raptures of a dream,
But for that streak—that deep and crimson streak—
Those gory spots,—what answer do they speak ?
'Tis Death, pale Death, you gaze upon—not sleep !
Yes ! Death—why start ye so ? gaze on and weep.

## PART OF AN UNFINISHED POEM.

I AM the youngest son of five,
Who am the only one alive.
My brothers four died at the stake,
Sooner than their freedom take,
By owning what their souls abhorr'd :
They perish'd of their own accord
Praying with their latest breath
For the foes who caus'd their death.
All have perish'd, all but one
   Whose years are full three score ;
And when his earthly course is run
   My father's race is o'er.
And I am he, the sole last link
   Of an unsullied chain,
And when the time comes, and I sink,
   Not one will then remain.
My father was a hunter bold,

A hardier could not be,
And many a tale could I unfold
　　How brave a man was he.
He track'd the wild boar to his lair,
Aud sought with eager steps the bear ;
For he was of an iron mood
　　With figure tall and strong ;
And many a night hath he pursued
　　His game the rocks among.
But wherefor he forsook a creed
For one which he was doom'd to bleed
　　I never learn'd or knew.
Enough it was that he became
In worship, as in thoughts, the same
　　As the protesting few.
The little hamlet where we dwelt
Was girdled by a rocky belt
　　Of mountains capp'd with snow ;
And at their base a river roll'd
Its heavy waters deep and cold
　　With stately pomp and slow.
But in the winter months it flows
When swollen with the melting snows
　　With a terrific sweep,
And all night long I've heard it roar

Like thunder near our cottage door
　　Till I have sunk to sleep ;
And sometimes, mingled with its sound,
The howling wolves were heard around
　　With tongues athirst for blood,
Compell'd by hunger and by cold
　　To leave their solitude,
And prowl around, gaunt, grim and bold
　　In savage search for food.
At other times I've heard the crash
Of thunder, and the lightning's flash
　　Lit up my lonely room,
And then the mountains have replied
And cast their echoes far and wide
　　Athwart the deep'ning gloom ;
And then each cliff and toppling rock
Hath quiver'd with the mighty shock,
As if the very earth was rent
Asunder by the element;
And many a monarch of the wood
Hath not the lightning's blast withstood,
The kingly oak, who vainly proud
Would dare the vengeance of the cloud
Hath had his hoary branches torn,
And all his native beauty shorn,

And when the thunder's died away
The winds have taken up the fray,
And lifted up the boiling river
Athwart two rocks that frown for ever—
Two shatter'd rocks that stand apart,
Thro' which the summer-tide would dart,
But now are hidden far below
Beneath the mad'ning river's flow,
And there about a furlong's space
Arose my father's dwelling place,
Perch'd on a gentle plot of ground
The prettiest spot of all around.
We had a little garden there
That own'd my father's private care.
Amid the waste it seem'd to stand
Like an oasis in the sand ;
And there I spent my youthful years—
That happy epoch without tears,
Ere the young mind had learn'd to know
That earthly joys are masks of woe,
That the bubbles on a river
Dancing on their giddy way ;
That the rainbow shadows ever
Sinking into swift decay
Are more stable far than they.

# THE VISION.

## A SONNET.

A STRANGE weird vision once mine eyes did view :
  Methought a shape of beauty touched my sight
  Like the still music of an opal's light.
His aspect shone with a celestial hue,
And locks all glistening with ambrosial dew ;
  His limbs were 'parell'd in a robe so bright
  That the swift rays of solitary Night
Slid melting from their beauty, as he drew
Near to my couch, until I could no more
  Restrain the impulse of a new-born fear ;
  But cried aloud " Oh wherefore art thou here ?"
It vanish'd, and I saw upon the floor
  A human skeleton in dark decay,
  Touch'd by the beams of the awakening day.

K

# APOLLO:

### A SONNET.

HIGH on a mount of Lebanon he stands
   A form of light and purity; awhile
   The fresh rob'd earth enraptur'd drinks his smile,
That from his lips of loveliness expands.
Supremely calm, he gazes o'er the lands
   Stretching afar, and many a blissful isle,
(Whose treasur'd stores no mortals yet defile)
While a bright harp sleeps in his glowing hands.

His glittering car of sunbeams hovers near,
   Drawn by two steeds with fiery wings endow'd,
   That fling strange music from each bursting cloud,
And thrill to ecstacy each listening sphere.
   Swiftly he mounts his glorious throne; while Night
   Shrinks trembling from his intense rays of light.

# LIFE AND DEATH.

## STANZAS.

WHAT is this death ? Is it a dreamless sleep,
   A dark unfathom'd slumber, and the mind
A living atom floating in the deep
   (Profundity of ether unconfin'd)
Until that day, when it again shall leap
   Into a form by Providence assign'd ;
The likeness of the form when in the clay
It had assum'd, before it passed away?


And what is life so wondrous, yet so frail ?
   Where are we mortals drifting ? From afar
We see but darkness and our strength would fail,
   But Hope's bright beacon glitters like a star :
We battle on tho' winds and storms assail
   Our slender barks with a terrific war.
While still the foaming surge of Time doth roll,
And bears us on ; for we have no control.

On, on we sweep amid the roar and hiss
    Of Time's unswerving stream ; while all around
The darkness of a bottomless abyss
    Enwraps the shore where we are swiftly bound.
On, on we sweep to torments or to bliss ;
    And all our cries of agony are drowned
Within the roar and bustle of the world.
On, on we sweep in one wild vortex hurl'd.

# SEA NYMPHS.

## A SONNET.

THEIR lovely forms lay shining on the strand :
  A twinkling group of sunbeams pure and bright,
  Sweet lipp'd and sleek their round breasts beamed with
     light ;
While their warm limbs in melting curves expand
With rosy shades entinctured, and each hand
  Shone with a starlike splendour to my sight.
  The air flash'd with their beauty, and the white
Snow-crested waves crept noiseless to the land.


I watched them till the sun sank to his home,
  All weaving crowns of rainbows for their hair,
Caught from the tangles of the fresh-spun foam ;
  'Till Amphitritè rising from her lair
Stole o'er the waves and charmèd them to sleep,
  Then softly slid they to their native deep.

## To J. R. T.

THE swift lights die from out the sky,
  The dusky shadows flutter.
Alone I brood in solitude
  O'er dreams I cannot utter.
I watch the distant ships float by,
  I hear the moaning sea,
And swiftly like some wild birds fly
  Sweet yearning thoughts to thee;
With arrowy spears the light-house peers
  Athwart the deep deep main ;
The soft dew floats in misty boats
  To anchor on the plain ;
The corn-craik sends from yonder lea
  Mementos sharp and shrill,
Which pierce the hoarse notes of the sea
  To break along the hill.

And thou, my friend, who art so dear,
My thoughts to thee still glide—
I look around, thou art not here—
I miss thee from my side.

## FAIRY LAND.

I TOUCH the strand of fairy land
  All brimming o'er with fancies;
I see the glades and colonnades
  Where light wing'd zephyr dances.
I saunter near the glassy mere;
  I breathe the scented flowers,
And sharp lights shoot from luscious fruit
  That reel to earth in showers.
I haunt the fountain's magic brim
  Where drowsy foam bells tinkle
To Nymphs that sleek with golden limb
  Each saucy dewlipp'd wrinkle.
I watch the lights that glance and gleam
  Shot from the cascade's glory.
I wander near the rapid stream
That darts along with melting song
  Near caverns dark and hoary.

And nightingales enchant the vales
  And Cupids float and flutter,
And from each scar of mountains far
  Shy Echoes breathe a mutter.
Each step I take new charms awake
  To woo me to fresh blisses;
My spirit reels, now music steals
  From charmèd wildernesses;
Now shy nymphs creep from lidded sleep
  And cast on me sly glances;
And from yon bourne a laughing Faun
  All nimble-footed dances.
But lo! a bell tolls the death knell
  To all my sweet romances,
Once more, ah me! Reality
  Dissolves my fairy fancies.

## A SONNET.

NIGHT after night a shuddering fear has crept
 Thro' my still breast, while thinking of that day
 When spectral shapes shall haunt again their clay,
To stand before that Holy One, who wept
Undying tears, while his disciples slept ;
 Of when the hearse shall bear my corpse away,
 For the cold worms to revel on their prey,
And to oblivion sinks my name, except
 By those whose spirits are enlocked in mine.
Will my departed spirit, freed from sin,
 Rejoicing hear those loving words divine—
" Thou good and faithful servant enter in,"
 Or like a knell of thunder hear Him say
 " Depart from hence to darkness and dismay ?"

## MUSIC.

FLING forth the notes in a swift melting stream,
Give me a deep draught of rich melody's cream,
Till I reel and am madden'd and thirsting would die
Drown'd in an ocean of ecstacy.

Faster, oh faster, I'm drunk as with wine ;
My bosom is bursting with rapture divine.
O for the plumes of an angel to soar
And float in ambrosial sounds evermore !

Oh words ye are feeble ! oh hush ye ! for now
Creeps one long plaintive fancy delicious and low ;
Soft melting like slumber it passes from sight
Too pure for aught earthly ; for mortals too bright.

Now bursts forth a shower—a thick mazy throng
Of full perfect notes, wing'd, dazzling and strong,
And madden'd with rapture they soar into air
With a wail of sweet cadence deep drawn with despair.

Ah now broods a silence ! then stately there flow
(Like a band of pale martyrs, sad, solemn and slow)
Notes born with a passion, which tremble and sigh
To ease their sweet breath ere they quiver and die.

O Music ! O Music ! Enchantress divine !
Sweet Mistress of solace I bend at thy shrine.
O'erwhelmed with emotion, my heart with thy power
Is thrill'd and expanded like a dew-fondled flower.

# THE BRIDE: AN ITALIAN ROMANCE.*

THERE is the swell of music soft and sweet
To festal songs and hum of busy feet,
Clear mellow voices mingle on the air
From happy beings beautiful and fair.
There is the pomp of revelry, the gleam
Of jewels bright, like sunbeams on a stream ;
And perfumes soft are mingling with the fall
Of waters, breathing freshness over all
The eager guests assembled in the hall.
And yet e'en there where all seems joy and pride
Beats one sad heart,—'tis thine, unhappy bride !
Link'd to a man whose heart must never know,
Thy hand has gone where thy love ne'er can go ;
The same old tale, an only daughter sold
In virgin purity for sordid gold,—
A daughter bending to her sire's decree,
And loving one she never more must see.

*One of the Author's early productions.

All gaze with admiration as with slow
And mournful steps she wanders to and fro.
A flashing shield of jewels bright and rare—
Her father's gift—adorns her raven hair ;
No other ornaments their lustre fling,
Save on her finger gleams her wedding ring,
Plac'd on by him whose very touch did fill
Her shrinking bosom with an icy chill.
Rob'd in pure white she moves along the hall,
The loveliest, yet the saddest of them all.
The streaming light, the scents, the music's strain,
Serve but to dazzle and confuse her brain.
The blaze of ornaments, the whirling throng,
The hum of laughter and the festal song,
The flashing arms, the snow-white bosoms bare,
Serve but to make more deep her sad despair.
With silent footsteps and with lovely grace
She turns to leave the festival, her face
White as the foam, which sparkling near, throws out
A dewy freshness o'er the giddy rout,
And then a sigh of sorrow or despair
Bursts from her lips as the calm midnight air
Play'd softly on her temples, and her eye
Filled with one tear.

The night was calm, the sky
Serenely beautiful, the moon shone bright
And over all shed forth a mellow light,
Reflecting bright the image of her sphere
A placid lake unrolls its waters near.
The music, now more distant, lost its wild
O'er whelming tones, and came in murmurs mild,
And all was solemn : not a leaf was stirr'd
By the calm air, nor faintest sound was heard ;
But all was buried in a deep repose.
She stands in silence, while her dark eye grows
Dim with a strange, fond yearning, and again
Bursts forth a sigh. The music chang'd its strain—
A low, sweet melody, sublimely clear,
By distance soften'd, caught her listening ear.
She started, for she knew that strain—'twas one
She oft had play'd to *him* ; but now its tone
Sank on her heart (already crush'd with care)
Like icy drops, and swiftly from their lair
Fierce scalding tears burst forth beyond control.
She did not try to check them, for her soul
Heav'd with an intense passion, and her frame
Shook with emotions which she could not tame.
A flood of thoughts came rushing like the wind,
And awful shapes with aspects undefin'd ;

Her marriage vows came ringing in her ear,
Her father's words, her husband's icy sneer,
The organ pealing forth its notes of praise,
The altar's dazzling light, the eager gaze
Of multitudes, the garlands and the flowers,
The hum of many voices, and the showers
Of pearly rice, the sweep of bridal dresses,
The laughing eyes, her maiden's soft caresses,
And above all the form of *one* shone bright
Like the pale moon amid the stars of night—
One manly form whom as she passed by said
" I wish thee happiness, my hopes are fled,
But thine,"—— no more she heard.    The glittering
      stream
Mov'd slowly on ; ah ! little did they deem
What fearful thoughts were surging thro' her breast
Of dazzling loveliness, ne'er to find rest,
What horrid things were floating thro' her brain
As she swept on, the loveliest of the train.

Oh what a sight to see her standing there !
Burning with love, with anguish and despair ;
The stars above, the lake's calm waters clear,
Tinged with the streaks of morning breaking clear,
And the long leaves which on the grey boughs sleep,
Flinging dim shadows o'er its bosom deep.

All, all are calm in heaven, earth and air,
Save in that breast—what tumults wild are *there !*


Meanwhile within, where all is life and pleasure,
Bright forms are moving to the music's measure,
And eyes are sparkling like the stars above,
And cheeks are blushing to the tones of love ;
Both youth and age are floating thro' the dance
Like stately clouds, while beams full many a glance
Which ne'er will be forgotten, and the touch
Of joyful hands which ling'ring, means so much ;
And hearts are beating with a secret pride
At dazzling looks and glances caught aside,
And whisper'd tones are answer'd by the gleam
Of smiling lips as bright as lover's dream,
And all is joy; or if a thought lurks there
Which should not be amid a scene so fair,
No languid sign betrays its dwelling place ;
For dazzling smiles are wreathing every face.
But lo ! a sudden movement of surprise,
And there are quivering lips and straining eyes ;
There is a strange commotion, and the trance
Of music breaks the spirit of the dance,
And there are clusters of the guests, who hear
A word which fills the gayest minds with fear,

L

And lo! there steals a whisper, which the tide
Of feverish hearts have caught, 'tis of the Bride.
Where can she be?  Full many an hour has past
Since their admiring eyes beheld her last.
Her father now is there with face as white
As the soft robes which flash upon his sight;
Her husband, too, with troubled air is speaking
While anxious guests the missing one are seeking,
And all is in a state of awe and fear,
And many an eye is glistening with a tear,
When lo! a servant enters, and the trace
Of recent tears are noticed on her face,
With hurried words her message she has said
And many caught those fearful words—"she's dead!"


There is the sound of weeping and strange cries,
And the bright lamps are showing streaming eyes;
The pomp of revelry is turn'd to gloom,
And horrid shrieks are heard from every room;
And he—the husband—who had sneering bought
Her lovely form with gold he wanted not,
What thinks he now? and he, the father, who
Had sold his only child—what thinks he too?
And they, the guests who envied, flattered, bow'd.
Behold them now, a wild distracted crowd;

And she is dead! they found her in the lake,
Pale, cold and still amid the feathery brake;
Her long silk tresses, where bright jewels gleam,
Lay darkly beautiful; and you might deem
She was in slumber, but for that cold brow,
That vacant eye, which loving, gleams not now;
But for that pale and moveless aspect, where
A tenderness half mingles with despair,
But soften'd all with langour, which has given
A calm repose, a rapture caught from heaven.
Ah! you can weep, but weeping will not bring
The bloom of life to that frail silent thing.
You sold her, but stern death hath snapt the claim—
No more she feels the bitterness of shame.

# THE OCEAN.

I CANNOT think where'er I go that I shall ever be
As happy as the time when I first sailed upon the sea.
'Tis true since then my foot has trod the deck full many a
time ;
And I have gaz'd o'er many a scene on many a foreign
clime ;
But never have my spirits rose with such wild throbs of
glee
As when at first upon me burst the billows of the sea.


I can recall with rapture still when first I heard the roar
Breath'd by the waves as awfully they dash'd upon the
shore ;
I can remember still with pride, when from an upland lea
I stood and gaz'd in solitude upon the swelling sea.
But never now within my breast such joyful feelings leap
As when I heard the wild sea-bird and roll'd upon the deep.

Ah ! many changes have ta'en place, my parents now are
    dead,
And many a hope is blotted out and many a joy is fled ;
And I have felt the chast'ning touch of anguish and of
    grief ;
And I have wept a thousand times and never found relief :
And Fortune too has chang'd her face ; her smiles are not
    for me
Since first I view'd in solitude the billows of the sea.


But still with joy I love to hear the mighty ocean roar
And watch his foaming billows break in thunder on the
    shore.
And if my bosom ne'er can know those impulses of glee
I yet can feel a pleasure steal when gazing on the sea.

## REMEMBER OR FORGET?

A SONNET

COMPOSED BY A LADY FRIEND, AGED FIFTEEN.

WHICH wilt thou do—remember or forget?
  Oh that I could but think the former, dear ;
That thou wilt shed a solitary tear
  When brooding o'er the past with fond regret.
But oh! I would not have thee ceaseless fret,
  Nor cause thy life to be unjoyful here ;
  Let loving memories man our bark and steer
For yonder isle where suns shall never set.

And when, alas! I've breathed a long adieu
  To beauteous England and her shadowy fells ;
  When I have ta'en my last fond look on thee,
And we are drifting o'er the ocean blue
  Unto a distant clime where Freedom dwells,
  Wilt thou in prayer remember those at sea ?

## GORDON.

ALONE upon the ramparts the dauntless warrior stands,
His heart is sad and heavy as he gazes o'er the sands.
The full round moon now at her height a flood of lustre
    throws
Detecting to his thoughtful glance the campments of his
    foes ;
No more is heard the murmur which at eventide arose
When their wild prophet chieftain in his savage robes
    array'd
Lifted up his impious hand and for *his* life's-blood pray'd.
But now the prayer is over and not a sound is heard
Except the drowsy locust's hum and sentinel's watchword.
Not distant far the swelling Nile glides calmly on its way
And o'er his head the spangled robes of midnight out-
    stretched lay.
And as he silent gazes there, what distant scenes arise,
And to his own dear native shore his noble spirit flies.

But has she then deserted him ?—the thought ends with a
sigh.

He will not think that Englishmen would leave a mate to
die

Alone, alone upon the sands without his comrades nigh.

No, no, 'tis past ! the doubt is gone that flush'd his cheeks
with shame—

He cannot think that Englishmen would stain their
country's name.

Alas for thee thou brave one, thy life was thrown away

By craven hearts who flatter'd thee, but flatter'd to betray.

And these are men whom Britons trust alas ! my native
shore—

Are all thy laurels to be rent thy children won of yore?

## IMAGINARY LINES

### SUPPOSED TO HAVE BEEN WRITTEN BY CHATTERTON

### IN ONE OF HIS PAROXYSMS OF DESPAIR.

How long, Oh God ! must I remain the tool,
The butt and jest of every babbling fool?
My mind is charg'd with feelings they ne'er knew,
And yet, forsooth, my haughty soul must sue :
Sue to be heard by men whom I despise
Who pay for wisdom with a pack of lies.
This cannot last, my frame is strangely worn
(No food has pass'd these lips since yester morn)
And where the next will come from—Heaven knows !
And while I starve the world laughs at my woes.
Oh dream of Fame ! thy smiles are but deceit,
Thy crown is death, thou flatters't but to cheat ;
Even now thou would'st (fair temptress)—but away—
No more shalt thou my foolish soul betray.

Despair—despair ! I love thee, hated thing ;
Thy cursed pangs shall be the theme I sing.
Come thou in all thy gloomy mantle drest.
This breast of mine well suits a horrid guest.
The world I hate—its juggling fools defy
I cannot live—Thank God ! I still can die.
And what is Death ? 'tis but a sudden rent
Thro' which the soul finds its own element,
The dissolution of this lump of clay
Born but to die and dying to decay.
If this be so, oh ! wherefore should I shrink
Back to this earth and shun the poisoned drink ?
Heroes have gone before me.  Wherefore wait
To be cut off by the sharp sword of fate ?
If Death is but the stillness of the heart
Why at the thought should every muscle start ?
Is there aught real in this ? 'tis but the thought
That thus recoils from what itself has wrought,
Fearing to leap in darkness from its mould
Into a realm whose secrets are untold.

## SONG TO THE FROST.

Swift spirit of the boundless air
  That wrinkles earth with seeds of ice,
And robes the branches lone and bare
  With mantles of a quaint device.

Thou sharpenst the stars with a keener light
  And the skies with a deeper blue,
And thou stiffenst the streams that sang all night
  With shackles all glistening and new.

Thou art the offspring of the cloud
  That faints from thy cold embrace,
And sinking to earth in a snowy shroud
  Lies gazing on heav'n with a passionless face.

Thou touchest the buds with thy fingers sharp
  Till they quiver, and droop, and die ;
And thou piercest the dry incrusted warp
  Where the innocent wheat seeds lie.

But thy reign is o'er when the dazzling sun
  In glorious splendour looks forth,
And viewing the ravage thy cold breath has done
  Drives thee back to thy home in the north.

## ISAAC WALTON.

### A SONNET.

PRINCE of all anglers ! I have dearly loved
 Thee and thy sport ; and oft my feet have stray'd
 To where some brook a fitting spot has made,
And there the pleasures of the rod have proved ;
Alert with joy if but the light quill moved
 By the soft touch of ripples slightly swayed—
 While small birds by my presence undismay'd,
Brimming with song all innocently roved.

Oh gentle lover of a sport divine !
 Haunter of Nature ! Comrade of the brook !
Immortal teacher of the rod and line !
 I feel the freshness of thy thoughtful book
Flow to my heart, (crush'd by the city's sway)
 Like some soft breeze rich with the scent of may.

# SHIPS AT SEA.

### A SONNET.

(This sonnet and the following one were written in competition with a friend who
was my guest at the sea-side.)

YE white rob'd beings of the trackless deep,
  Whose motion is the shadow of repose ;
  Churning old Ocean's dimples into snows
Of flashing foam and waves which swiftly leap
Like the wild cubs of lions fast asleep,
  Awakened by the slopings of your prows.
  Ye seem like things untouch'd by earthly woes—
Creatures that slumber as ye onward sweep.

So calm ye move ye scarcely seem to glide,
  And yet I feel that ye will soon be gone,
Rob'd in the trappings of your swan-like pride,
  Tracking the footsteps of yon sinking sun.
Ah ! now ye seem to hover near the sky.
Farewell to ye ! I watch ye with a sigh.

A. A. D. B.

## SHIPS AT SEA.

### A SONNET.

WE WALKED abroad this bleak March afternoon
  On yon tall cliff, and saw each full-sail'd ship.
  Their strong, sharp prows thro' clearest wavelets dip;
And lovely gleam'd they 'neath the smile of noon.
Oft when at evening shone the clear cold moon
  I've watch'd them, or when from old Boreas' lip
  A tempest broke, and by his clenching grip
Held their stout hearts in terror wild; and soon,
By his kind will—not daring to destroy—
  The sea was tamed, and peacefully they went,
No longer tossed by the wild wind's annoy,
  But by a gentle breath; and they were sent
Along their liquid paths rejoicingly,
Glad in the glory of the boundless sea.

J. R. T.